Prairie Brides

This Large Print Book carries the Seal of Approval of N.A.V.H.

Prairie Brides:
Book One

The Bride's Song
Linda Ford

The Barefoot Bride
Linda Goodnight

Thorndike Press • Waterville, Maine

Copyright © 2000 by Linda Ford.
Copyright © 2000 by Linda Goodnight.

All Scripture quotations are taken from the King James Version of the Bible.

All rights reserved.

Published in 2005 by arrangement with Barbour Publishing, Inc.

Thorndike Press® Large Print Christian Fiction.

The tree indicium is a trademark of Thorndike Press.

The text of this Large Print edition is unabridged.
Other aspects of the book may vary from the original edition.

Set in 16 pt. Plantin by Al Chase.

Printed in the United States on permanent paper.

Library of Congress Cataloging-in-Publication Data

Prairie brides. Book one / by Linda Ford and Linda Goodnight.
    p. cm. — (Thorndike Press large print Christian fiction)
  ISBN 0-7862-7723-8 (lg. print : hc : alk. paper)
    1. Love stories, American. 2. Women pioneers — Fiction.
3. Nurses — Fiction. 4. Widows — Fiction. 5. Frontier and pioneer life — Fiction. 6. Historical fiction, American.
7. Kansas — Fiction. 8. Large type books. I. Ford, Linda. Bride's song. II. Goodnight, Linda. Barefoot bride.
III. Thorndike Press large print Christian fiction series.
PS648.L6P725 2005

2005008225

Prairie Brides

National Association for Visually Handicapped
serving the partially seeing

As the Founder/CEO of NAVH, the only national health agency solely devoted to those who, although not totally blind, have an eye disease which could lead to serious visual impairment, I am pleased to recognize Thorndike Press* as one of the leading publishers in the large print field.

Founded in 1954 in San Francisco to prepare large print textbooks for partially seeing children, NAVH became the pioneer and standard setting agency in the preparation of large type.

Today, those publishers who meet our standards carry the prestigious "Seal of Approval" indicating high quality large print. We are delighted that Thorndike Press is one of the publishers whose titles meet these standards. We are also pleased to recognize the significant contribution Thorndike Press is making in this important and growing field.

Lorraine H. Marchi, L.H.D.
Founder/CEO
NAVH

* Thorndike Press encompasses the following imprints: Thorndike, Wheeler, Walker and Large Print Press.

The Bride's Song

Linda Ford

Introduction

The Bride's Song by Linda Ford
Dora Grant isn't cut out to be a pioneer and despises the homesteader's existence. She is content with her nursing job in a small Canadian town. But when a cowboy with bold dreams of heading west becomes her patient, Dora is forced to reevaluate her clutch on comforts and security. Is love worth the risks?

Chapter 1

1898 — Freebank, western Canada

A gust of wind swept shiny strands of black hair across Dora Grant's cheek as she hastened across the pleasant, tree-lined street. Lifting her face into the wind, she laughed. At twenty-two she had found the ideal place and she was supremely happy.

The prosperous town of Freebank was the perfect place for a determined young woman to carve out a life for herself. Situated alongside the Canadian Pacific rail line, which headed west to free land, opportunity, and prosperity, the thriving community boasted of schools, over twenty stores, six churches, a theater, and an abundant social life.

Climbing the three stairs to Doc Mackenzie's office, Dora stepped inside. She smiled at her reflection as she paused at the hall table to brush her hair back from her face. Her hazel eyes sparkled, revealing her happy state of mind. With deft movements, she tied a crisp white apron over her skirt and blouse. She had changed her mind about wearing her new white lawn blouse this morning, deciding to do the wise thing and save it for a social occasion. Her plain, oft-worn apparel was more appropriate for work.

Her footsteps kept pace with the happy tune she hummed as she completed her routine morning chores. Placing freshly boiled instruments on a tray, she covered them with a clean towel.

If Doc Mackenzie doesn't get back soon, he won't have time for his noon meal, she thought when she glanced at the clock over the bookcase. Perhaps she should go into the living quarters and sit with Mrs. Mac until the doctor returned. But before she could cross the room, a buggy rattled into the yard followed almost immediately by Doc's heavy footfall on the stoop.

Instantly, her anxious wonderings eased. Doc would get a chance to eat the simple meal she'd left for Mrs. Mac to serve. Now, Dora could relax until their afternoon office hours began.

But the racket of a fast-approaching wagon sent tickling fingers of apprehension up her spine.

"Whoa," a deep voice called out, followed

by a frantic inquiry. "Doc. Doc Mackenzie. Are you home?"

Dora hurried to the window, pushing aside the lace curtain. Two heaving and sweating horses stood harnessed to a wagon that still shuddered from its sudden halt. Her gaze followed two men as they jumped down from their seats and reached back into the wagon's bed to lift out a blanket-wrapped body.

The driver gave the reins a quick twist as he leapt to the ground. "Doc," he hollered again. "Injured man here." He hurried to assist the other two.

Dora's heart dipped for an instant before she sprang to the door. Poor Doc would be missing his meal again.

"Bring him in," she instructed the trio of men as they staggered up the steps with their burden. "Doc will be here right away." Dora half extended her hand but quickly pulled it back and stepped out of the way when she saw the extent of the injuries.

"You're sure he's still alive?" At the sound of Doc's familiar voice, her head spun toward the door leading to the living quarters. Doc wiped his mouth on his hanky as he entered the office. Had he grabbed a mouthful of food or only managed a hurried drink? But there was no time to think about

Doc's eating requirements.

"He ain't kicking much but he's still breathing," one man grunted.

"Right here." Dora led the men to an examining table.

Doc flipped aside the blanket and bent over the patient. "A bit battered up, are we?" With deft fingers he lifted the eyelids then bent closer to examine the cut on the forehead. "Dora, give me a hand."

Immediately, she was at the doctor's side. Her breath caught for one fleeting second, but she had worked with Doc long enough to know how to closely observe blood, injuries, pain, and death while still maintaining her composure.

There were a number of bruises on the injured man's face. A head wound oozed over crackled patches of dried blood. The left side of the man's shirt was stained dark red. He was deathly still and pasty-white.

The dark spot on his shirt grew.

She shook her head. No telling how much damage was hidden under the torn garment, yet his chest fell and rose with assuring regularity.

"You boys going to tell me what happened?" Doc flashed the trio a glance as Dora unbuttoned the shirt and slipped it from the man's shoulders. Doc probed the kidney area and across the abdomen then pushed the edges of the wound together.

"We found him," the driver answered.

"Thought he was dead," mumbled the younger man as he removed his hat and shuffled his fingers along the rim.

Doc snorted. "Where did you find him?"

"Across the river. About ten miles away." Again it was the driver who supplied the information.

"He was passed out, sittin' in his saddle."

"Just like he was dead." The hat went round and round.

"Shut up, Jack." The third man straightened. "He gonna be okay, Doc?"

"You boys get the sheriff and tell him everything, you hear?" Doc said, casting a glare in their direction. "Now run along so we can take care of him."

Dora smiled. Doc might be getting a little round in the middle and his hair might be gray and thinning but, on occasion, he looked and sounded like an army major and received the same instant obedience. She didn't wait for their noisy exit before she filled a basin with warm water. Pulling the tray of instruments close, she began dabbing at the blood.

She worked quietly. Doc didn't care for idle conversation. Her movements coordinated with his as he cleaned and stitched the wounds.

Before the men returned, the patient had been washed and eased into a clean gown. Twice he had moaned and tried to say something before fading back into unconsciousness.

At the sound of shuffling boots, Doc straightened. "They're just in time to help get this young man into bed." He washed and dried his hands before he opened the door to the outer office.

"Come in, Constable." The local Mountie entered, closing the door on the others.

Constable Andrews yanked his hat off as he stared down at the injured man. "He say anything?"

"No. He's a lucky young man to even be alive." Doc lifted the patient's eyelids again. "Can't tell how serious this head wound is." Straightening, he faced the RCMP officer. "There's not much more I can do."

The Mountie nodded. "They brought in his horse and tack." He sighed. "I hoped he'd be able to tell me what happened."

"In good time, my man. In good time." Doc hustled to the door. "Now if you and these gentlemen could give me a wee bit of help, we'll see this lad settled into bed."

Minutes later the patient rested in the sickroom off the office, and the room was cleared of nervous men. Doc and Dora stood side by side staring down at the man.

"He's a bonnie young man." Doc lapsed into his Scottish brogue. "He'll be turning heads on many a young lass."

Dora blinked then looked intently at the patient. Dark curls lay flattened across his head. Despite his paleness and bruises, he *was* handsome — in a rugged sort of way.

But his clothing had revealed his occupation. A cowboy. Decisively, Dora shook her head. "Not this lass."

Doc chuckled. "No, my bonnie lassie. You're knowing what you want and how to get it."

She laughed too. "No wandering cowboy for me."

Office hours over, Dora shooed Doc away for a meal and some much needed rest before dragging a chair to the bedside of her patient. She prepared to keep watch for a few hours.

The injured man tossed and moaned.

In response to his pain, Dora murmured soft, soothing assurances.

His eyes flew open, and she stared into brown eyes so velvety that her breath caught in her throat. The flicker of pain and confusion in those dark orbs quickly reminded her of her duties. "You're at Doc Mackenzie's. You have a cut on your head and another in your side, but you're safe now. If you lay quiet and rest, you'll soon be right as rain."

He flinched.

She offered her most encouraging smile. He could use something for pain, but she didn't dare leave him to fetch Doc. Besides, she knew Doc would be in shortly to check on his patient.

"Can you tell me your name?"

He groaned and his lips moved.

She leaned closer. It sounded like he said "Rivers." Was he trying to tell her what had happened?

But before she could formulate another question, his eyes closed. She leaned back in her chair, thankful that he hadn't grown more restless. A few minutes later, Doc entered the room.

"Any change?" He bent over the patient as he spoke.

"He opened his eyes for a moment."

Doc nodded, lifting a corner of the dressing on the man's side. "I'm not happy with the looks of this. Could you please get me a clean dressing, Dora?"

She hurried to do as he had asked and quickly returned to his side. Handing him a basin for the soaked bandage, Dora noticed the inflamed edges of the wound.

"Did he say anything?"

"Rivers."

"What does that mean?" Doc stared at her.

She shrugged. "Suppose he was trying to tell us something about where he got hurt."

Dora sat with the patient until late in the evening. The uninterrupted quiet gave her plenty of time to study his features. Doc was right. Many a young woman would throw this man a second look — and a third — while hoping for more. An unsettled feeling surfaced. A familiar feeling. Although she loved her work and where she lived, every once in awhile she wished she weren't so alone.

Doc came in. "Dora, you go get your rest now."

"But what about you?" she protested. Doc never got enough rest. When he wasn't caring for patients, he was tending to Mrs. Mac, who had grown weaker with each passing winter month. When hoped-for improvement did not materialize with the arrival of spring, Dora could no longer deny the truth; Mrs. Mac was not going to get stronger. This strange ailment, which had literally eaten the flesh from her frame and left her barely able to function, was not going away.

No wonder Doc looked tired most of the time. She wished she could do more to help this couple who had become as dear as any parents.

But, despite Dora's objections, Doc gently pushed her from the room.

"I plan on dozing in the big chair. The laudanum will take effect in a few minutes and our patient should sleep soundly."

With no other option but to follow the doctor's orders, Dora let herself out and hurried across the street to the little house she called her own. A sense of peace and satisfaction swept over her as she lit the kerosene lamp in the room that served as parlor, kitchen, and dining room. Tacked onto the back of the house was an equally small bedroom.

Would she ever enter this house or cross the street to the doctor's office without experiencing a swell of gratitude for God's wonderful provisions? Knowing she would not, her weariness lifted. A smile played on her lips as she murmured, "Thank you, God."

Her prayer of thanksgiving shifted to one of petition as she quietly spoke to the Lord. "... And, dear Father, please bless Doc and Mrs. Mac — and that poor injured man." Breathing a quick "Amen," Dora began to hum while she bustled about the kitchen, preparing tea and a plate of boiled egg sandwiches.

When Dora arrived for work early the next morning, she found Doc asleep in the chair. Noiselessly, she pulled the patient's door closed and headed for the office to prepare for the day's work. A bit later, upon hearing the murmur of voices, she returned to the sickroom.

Doc glanced up from his examination of the patient's abdominal wound. "Another dressing please."

As she passed a clean bandage to him, she saw how the lesion oozed.

Doc finished and straightened. "He's conscious now but I've just given him another laudanum." He handed the instruments to Dora and dipped his hands in the basin of water. "His name is Josh Rivers."

She smiled at her misunderstanding of the night before.

"He was set upon by two men who robbed him and beat him up, leaving him to die."

Doc dried his hands on a fresh, white towel. "But he refused to die." He handed the towel to Dora and stood over the patient, his expression serious. "He's got a fight ahead of him yet, I fear. I'll leave him in your care for now. I have house calls to make. Do your best to keep him quiet. I'll leave another dosage of laudanum, should he need it."

Before she could do more than nod her head in agreement, the doctor had gone.

The morning passed slowly. Mr. Rivers stirred several times but settled quickly when she touched him and spoke softly.

Doc returned prior to the afternoon office hours. "I'll manage without you in the office this afternoon." He touched Josh's brow. "I want you stay by our patient and keep a close eye on him."

Within an hour, Josh was burning with fever.

Dora poured rubbing alcohol into tepid water and sponged him. His life depended on her fighting the fever and keeping him as quiet as possible. She determined to do her very best. As always, she felt a fierce defiance at the illnesses and injuries that attacked her patients.

Doc came in later that afternoon to check the dressing. "Nasty injury," he exclaimed as he pulled the bandage away from the wound. "Let's apply a bread poultice and see if that draws out the infection."

Dora and Doc labored over Josh, his moans tearing at her as they fought the raging fever. Toward morning it abated and the patient fell into a deep sleep.

Dora sank into the chair and let her breath out in a whoosh, tired to the marrow of her bones.

"You run on home and catch some sleep," Doc commanded. She started to argue but he shooed her from the chair.

"Sleep as long as you need then come and take over — though, I'm hoping the worst is over. If we can keep him quiet a few days I believe he'll mend."

Dora still hesitated but Doc had already sunk into the chair, tucking a pillow under his head and stretching out his legs. He waved her away. She stole one more glance at Josh in order to assure herself that he was really and truly better. But she stilled the protective urge to feel his brow one more time before hurrying from the room.

Three hours later she awoke refreshed and, as always, anxious to check on her patient. If she felt a bit more urgency this time, she refused to admit it.

Doc slept in the chair, his head tilted to one side. "Doc," she whispered, "I'll take over." He moaned as he jerked to his feet and wearily plodded from the room.

Josh rested peacefully. She pressed her fingers to his brow and nodded. His fever had not returned. Dora lightly pushed at one brown curl that stubbornly hung over his forehead. The quiet of the house settled around her, and she relaxed into the cushiony softness of the big armchair.

"So you *are* real."

The voice shocked her bolt upright. Dora gaped at her patient, his warm brown eyes on her face, a smile tipping his lips.

"I thought I'd dreamed you." His voice was deep and slow as a lazy river. She found herself wondering if he always sounded like that or if it was the result of pain and drugs. Then she forced her attentions back to their proper place.

"Welcome back. How are you feeling?" *Certainly his color is improved,* she thought.

In response, he grimaced. "A little like I was run over by a stampede of longhorns."

She smiled. Awake and more alert, his eyes took on a life of their own, darkening with warmth then flashing with pain. She leaned over his bedside. "Can I get you something for the pain? Doc Mackenzie left a powder for you."

He closed his eyes. "The medicine will

make me sleep, won't it?"

"Yes."

"But I don't want to sleep." Jaw tightening, eyes flashing, he shot her a determined look. "I have things to do." Dora gasped as he tried to sit up. Instantly, he fell back against the pillow, his face chalk-white.

"You must lie still. You have a deep wound in your side that needs time to heal."

He grunted. "Time's one thing I ain't got. Where's my horse?"

"I heard the Mountie say he has your horse and gear."

"What about them rattlers that robbed me?" She shivered at the hard note in his voice.

"They were long gone."

"I gotta get going." He twisted his head from side to side.

"First, you must get better." Dora's lips tightened. If he kept this up, he would start to bleed again. Maybe she should give him the laudanum. What would Doc want?

As if in answer to her question, Doc strode in. "Well, what do we have here? Glad to see you looking alive, young man."

"Doc, I gotta get moving." Again, Josh attempted to sit up.

Doc pressed Josh's shoulders to the bed.

"Now you look here, young fella. You're mighty lucky to be alive. And I intend to see you well. Either you lie quiet until I say otherwise or I'll keep you so doped up you won't have any choice." He glared at Josh.

Josh met Doc's gaze. Neither spoke. Neither flinched.

Dora held her breath. Doc meant every word and he would not relent. She hoped Josh would see this and save himself a pack of trouble.

Josh suddenly relaxed and smiled. "You're the doctor," he announced, almost cheerfully.

Dora grinned. Not only did he have spirit, this man had brains. He would be a good patient.

Doc relaxed. "There's a good man." He patted Josh's shoulder. "Now let's have a wee look at that wound."

Dora hurried to get fresh bandages as Doc rolled back the dressing. Peering over his shoulder, she saw the edges of the wound were inflamed but not oozing, an improvement since yesterday.

Doc applied a new dressing. "You must keep still until this heals," he said as he washed his hands. "Dora, get the young man something to eat. Liquids for now." Scowling at Josh, he ordered, "You, young man, are to let Dora feed you. I want you absolutely still. Do you hear?"

Josh grinned. "I hear ya, Doc."

Doc snorted.

Josh's quick flash of humor was a pleasant treat after the many complaining patients she'd had over the winter, and Dora smiled as she headed toward the kitchen.

Mrs. Mac sat at the table, toying with her empty teacup.

"How are you today, Mrs. Mac?"

"I'm managing." Her hand shook as she brushed a strand of white hair back. "But I worry about Ian when he works such long hours."

Dora nodded. Doc's hours were long and doing nursing duty added to them. But there was no other doctor. And Doc would not ignore someone needing medical attention. She tried to put in some time every day helping Mrs. Mac with housework and meals, but Doc had made it clear that her duties as his nurse came first and she understood it had to be so.

"I'll clean the kitchen while I wait for the water to boil." She quickly put away the food then gathered and washed the dishes. Mixing a spoonful of beef concentrate with hot water in a bowl, she wrinkled her nose at the smell. She'd make some real chicken broth later, but for now this would have to do.

"Thank you, dear," Mrs. Mac said as Dora put away the last dish and prepared the tray.

"You're welcome. I wish I had time to do more, but Doc has ordered me to feed our patient." She checked the tray. Tea, sugar, if he desired, and weak bouillon. Not much for a young man. Imagining how he would feel about his liquid meals, she grimaced.

Yet her lips changed to a smile as she entered the sickroom.

"Good, you're back." Doc stood, pulling his jacket straight. "Keep him on clear fluids today and keep him still. I don't care how. Give him laudanum if necessary."

He made it sound near impossible but she would not disappoint him. "I understand."

Doc fixed his glare on Josh. "I expect your full cooperation, young man."

"Doc, relax. I'll be a good boy. I promise I won't move a muscle until you say it's safe." He sighed. "I'm sure hoping you don't mean not moving my mouth though. I'd have a hard time keeping it shut for very long."

Doc snorted. "Flap your jaws all you want, sonny. Won't do you any harm." He dipped his head toward Dora. "Might drive your nurse crazy, though."

Dora lifted her chin. " 'Spect he can't be any worse than some of the people I've put up with."

Doc chortled at Josh's groan. He was still chuckling as he left the room.

Ignoring him, she asked Josh, "How about some nourishment?" Then, she pushed another pillow behind Josh's head before she pulled the tray close.

He eyed the cup and bowl suspiciously.

She hesitated. "Which would you like first, tea or broth?"

His gaze darted to her face in disbelief. "Does it make a difference?"

"Not to me," she answered cheerily, and lifting the bowl to his chin, she gave him a spoonful of bouillon.

He grimaced. "I've tossed better stuff than that in the fire."

Before he could say more, she fed him another spoonful. "Who says it's supposed to be good? All that matters is it's full of nutrition."

His eyes narrowed. "If it's awful, it must be good for me; is that what you're saying?"

She laughed. "I suppose I am."

He shook his head. "What a dreadful idea." He got a faraway look in his eyes. "Thank goodness life isn't like that. God has given us so much to enjoy. Like nature, friends, and . . ." He darted a look at the tray. "Good food."

She blinked. He had put into words a sentiment that had been flickering in the back of her mind for a long time. With all her heart she believed life was not *all* pain and disappointment. There was so much good to be enjoyed — gifts from a good and loving God. Like her home, her job, her life here in town. So many of life's unpleasantries were self-inflicted. She clenched her teeth, vowing, once again, not to make any of the same unwise and devastating choices that her parents had made.

"Ah sweet Dora, you should not look so sad."

She stifled a gasp. Heat raced up her neck. Such brashness. But she'd heard about wild cowboys.

He held both palms toward her. "Don't get all flustered. I'm not meaning to be bold."

She kept her head bent, unwilling to meet his gaze.

"Some of that tea would be good."

With a guilty start, she realized she had forgotten about feeding him. He downed the last of the broth and drank his tea, then nestled back into his pillow. Filled with an uncomfortable restlessness, she gathered up the utensils and tray and hurried to the kitchen. It was empty, and the house quiet. Doc had undoubtedly gone on his rounds and Mrs. Mac would be resting.

Dora quickly washed the dishes. Josh's remark about enjoying good things triggered her interest. Obviously, he was a God-fearing man. It might be amusing to get to know him. She bit her bottom lip. Too bad he was a cowboy.

When she returned to the sickroom, Josh lay with his eyes closed. Dora hesitated, but Josh sensed her presence and slowly opened his eyes. "Glad to see you back," he said with a smile. "I thought I might have scared you off and would have to spend the rest of the day staring at the walls." His eyes darkened. "I was thinking about going to find you."

Remembering Doc's orders, she shook her head. "Doc would have my skin if you did."

"I guess that means you have to entertain me then." The smug look on his face made her laugh.

"I'm not sure that's what he meant."

He sighed deep and long. "I feel like I've been hog-tied. All the while, my insides are yearning to move."

Dora made a cluck of sympathy. He had capitulated so completely to Doc's orders that she had failed to realize how much it cost him. Now her heart reached out to ease his restlessness. "What are you so anxious to be doing?"

His eyes brightened. "I'm headed west."

She closed her eyes for a heartbeat. Another fool after land and riches. Chasing an empty bubble. And just when she had decided that he thought the same as she.

"Why are you heading west?" As if she didn't know the answer. The lonely feeling that had surfaced earlier now returned, and she struggled to submerge the emotion. Life was good and pleasant. She would allow nothing to mar her happiness. Not after God had so generously provided.

"I'm going to find me the nicest piece of land ever and start my own little farm." His gaze drifted away and she knew he was seeing his own dream world.

She shook her head. How often she'd seen that look and heard that tone. Yet, even more often, she had seen the helpless desperation in a child's gaunt face. Her insides coiled and she pushed away the memories, forcing herself to concentrate on making conversation with her patient — this dreamer headed into the unknown with nothing by a headful of second-hand lies.

"Have you any idea what you're headed for?" She managed to keep her voice smooth and tried to ignore the unreasonable twinge in her heart.

"I've seen it. A few years ago I was trailing a herd to Cochrane Ranch. Prettiest country I ever saw. The air is so pure you can taste yesterday's rain. The moon was so big and golden I was sure it was snagged on a pine tree." He took a deep breath. "I never saw a sky so blue. Seemed like you could reach out and touch it." He turned to Dora with an eager look in his eyes. "You should have seen the flowers. Wild roses so sweet that I dreamed of them at night. Harebells like fine china." He grinned at Dora. "Why I bet you could hear them ringing if you sat real still."

Not certain what he meant, she stared at him. Then, seeing the twinkle in his eye, she laughed low in her throat. "Indeed?" she replied. "I don't believe I've ever heard the sound of harebells ringing."

He chuckled, beaming at her. "Me neither, but who knows. The country is dandy. So purdy — the land nearly sings." He lay back and stared at the ceiling. "I already knew that I didn't want to be trailing doggies the rest of my life. I made up my mind the minute I saw that little spot of heaven. I would work and save until I had enough to set me up in a nice little place of my own." He heaved a chest-raising sigh. "And just when I figured that the right time had come, I find myself laid up here."

She didn't answer. He made the west country sound like paradise on earth. She could almost hear the music and the bells he described. But she had seen another version of paradise, one with dark corners.

"Perhaps you've been given a warning . . ." At the sudden change in his expression she clamped her lips together.

"There you go again. Figuring bad things are good for you."

She wanted to argue. That was not what she had said, nor meant. But he drew his brows together and continued.

"Don't you think I've had plenty of time to think and pray about this?" The fierceness in his expression disappeared as quickly as it had come. "This is a delay. For what purpose, I have no notion. However, my aim is still the same."

Stung by his words, and even more by his judgment, she faced him squarely. "I suppose you know all about farming?"

"I've been keeping my eyes open, and I know enough to run myself a few cows and grow them some feed." He paused. "Besides, I learn quick."

Her annoyance fled as fast as it came. "I'm sorry," Dora offered, shrugging her shoulders. "It's none of my business. Perhaps I've seen too many people lose all they had in the trying."

He chuckled. "Maybe I'm a fool but I don't see I have much to lose."

Just then, Doc appeared to check on his patient and repeat his order for quiet and rest. A few minutes later Constable Andrews arrived to ask Josh a few questions and get his description of the two men who had attacked and robbed him. Before the Mountie left, he brought in a pair of saddlebags from the waiting room.

"I have no way of knowing what's missing, but I thought you might like to have your things at hand." He tossed the leather bags on the foot of the bed. "The rest of your tack is at the livery barn. You can pick it up there when you are able to be up and about."

Josh received his liquid meal with a wrinkled nose. When he had finished drinking his dinner, Dora insisted that her patient rest for a few hours. While he slept, she made a quick trip to the butcher shop and bought a stewing hen, which she put on the stove to simmer. After preparing a meal and dining with the Mackenzies, she helped Doc with his office patients. Despite her busyness, her mind kept returning to the sickroom and her patient. She hoped he was resting quietly and his wounds were healing.

Doc glanced at the door several times as well. "Hope the lad is obeying orders," he graveled under his breath between patients. But another rush of patients prevented either of them from checking on Josh.

"We're done now, Lass," Doc said as he closed the door on their last patient. "Go see how our cowboy is getting along."

Doc sat behind his desk and drew his heavy green ledger close. She hurried toward the sickroom, knowing that the doctor would be preoccupied for some time.

Chapter 2

She brushed a tendril of hair from her face and reached for the knob, then pulled back, not wanting to waken him if he were asleep. Turning the glass knob slowly, she eased the door open and tiptoed into the room.

The afternoon sun filtered through the lace curtains shooting bright light across the room and making it difficult to distinguish details. Before her eyes adjusted, Josh called out.

"Dora. Thank goodness. I thought no one was coming back." His voice rang with desperation. "Tell me, please. What is that gut-wrenching smell?"

She chuckled. "That would be Lister's spray. A disinfectant that keeps disease from spreading."

"I can believe that. No disease would want to get near such a stench!"

Her eyes had adjusted to the light and she gasped. "How did you get that stuff?" Items lay scattered across his bedside.

"From my saddlebag." He sounded apprehensive. "I was so bored." He grew defensive. "I barely had to move. Knew exactly where they were. Just had to reach out my toe and drag it close."

She shook her head. It would be a miracle if he hadn't started the wound bleeding again.

"You won't tell Doc will you? I promise I was very careful and didn't pull anything loose. Please, Dora, be a pal."

She looked away from his begging eyes. She knew she shouldn't agree to such a scheme, but she also knew that she would. For the life of her, she couldn't explain why.

"We'd better tidy up." She gathered up the items, surprised when she examined them more closely. Besides several rolled up pairs of socks and a new pair of leather gloves, there was a well-worn leather Bible, its cover as soft as velvet. He retrieved an equally worn book, *The Great Lone Land*, and a picture before she could pack them away.

He watched her, smiling gently. "Thanks a heap."

She straightened and smoothed the crazy-patch quilt, carefully avoiding his gaze — a gaze that somehow compelled her to do things she wouldn't normally agree to do.

Again, his voice softly pleaded. "Could I

ask one more favor?" His words made her feel that to refuse him would be mean.

She steeled herself. "You can ask."

He chuckled. "All I want is for you to open those curtains so I can enjoy the sunshine."

His request was so mundane that she had to laugh at her defensiveness as she crossed the floor to do his bidding. Light flooded the room when she pulled back the curtains. Turning back toward Josh, she observed a look of pure pleasure on his face as he lay with his eyes closed. She quickly turned away, for she felt as though she were intruding on someone in the midst of private prayer.

"Does the window open?"

"Certainly." She pushed the sash upward. A refreshing breeze, full of spring warmth and laden with the musky smell of recent winter snow, lifted the lace curtains to brush against her arms. Dora filled her lungs with fresh air.

The room was quiet. A child's voice sounded somewhere in the distance, and a horse clip-clopped down the street. Dora turned to look at Josh. In the bright light, his skin was even more tanned, a stark contrast to the bandage on his forehead. Gold streaks played through his brown curls.

As she studied him, his eyes opened. His expression warm, he said, "Now I can breathe." He smiled. "I've been looking at the picture of my family. See, here they are." He motioned for her to come to his side.

She looked down at the picture, still feeling the lure of the spring breeze.

Then she bent closer. "How many brothers and sisters do you have?" She hadn't meant to sound so startled.

"I'm the oldest of ten." There was no disguising his pride.

"These three," he explained, pointing to the smaller ones, "Ruthie, Tessa, and Mark were born after I left home. Ruthie's nine years old, Tessa's seven, and Mark just turned five."

Dora bent closer. "You're the eldest?" There seemed to be several adults in the photo.

"Firstborn. That's me. This . . ." With his index finger he pointed to a young man who bore a resemblance to Josh. "This is Andy. He's twenty-four. As soon as I saw he was keen on running the mill, unlike myself, I declared I was going to follow my dream. Ten years now I've been working, mostly as a ranch hand or trailing cows." He ran his finger back and forth across the picture.

"Good work. Good experience. But I'm ready to settle down and build something for myself. And someday, God willing, for my family."

Dora kept her head bent over the picture. These faces stirred an all-too-familiar feeling within her. The same old dream. The same empty hope she'd seen before. The lure of owning land and creating something for future generations to have and hold. So much hope. So much disappointment and despair. Such a waste. Finally she lifted her gaze to Josh. "Don't your parents need you at home?"

"There was barely enough of everything to go around. As we grew into adulthood it seemed there was less."

She narrowed her eyes, amazed that he seemed to feel no bitterness at such a lean existence.

"I go and visit whenever I can." He let his hands drop to his chest. The photo pointed toward the ceiling. "I spent a fortnight with them before I started west. Saying good-bye this time was harder than lassoing a racing bronc, knowing it might be a long while before I see them again." His thumb rubbed the photo. "The little ones will hardly remember me."

She clenched her hands into fists. Her insides screamed to tell him to give up this foolish chase. Instead, she took a deep breath and said, "I put a chicken on the stove to simmer several hours ago. Perhaps you'd like some homemade chicken broth."

He pressed his hands to his chest. "Dora, now I'm certain you're an angel of mercy. Sure you can't add some noodles or potatoes?"

She shook her head. "Not 'til Doc says so." She hesitated at the door. "I'll be back in a few minutes."

In the kitchen, Mrs. Mac stood at the table cutting meat from the chicken carcass.

Dora came up beside her. "Why thank you, Mrs. Mac." She reached out for the knife. "Here, let me finish."

Mrs. Mac nodded and relinquished the knife. "I'm feeling a little better this afternoon."

Dora pulled Mrs. Mac's arm through her own, leading her gently to a chair. "I'm glad."

"I think I'll get stronger with the warmer weather." She leaned heavily on the table as she sat down.

Dora poured tea for her and waited until she grasped the cup and took a sip before she turned back to the counter. She finished the deboning, then peeled potatoes and carrots for a stew for Doc and Mrs. Mac. Straining some broth for Josh's supper, she set aside the remainder and some diced meat. Doc would probably order soft food tomorrow. She would prepare some chicken noodle soup.

As she diced potatoes into the stew, Mrs. Mac asked, "How is your patient this afternoon?"

Dora glanced up and smiled. "He's on the mend but I think he finds being bedridden difficult." She shook her head. "But he must remain still if he wants that gash in his side to heal."

"Aye, this being idle is not a task to be envied."

Dora dropped the knife and hurried to the older lady's side, bending over to hug her. "Oh Mrs. Mac, you're not idle. You do what you can and that's all any of us can do."

Mrs. Mac patted Dora's hands and leaned against her shoulder. "Thank you, dearie. You're such a sweet lass. Makes me ashamed of me grumbling."

Before Dora could think of how to respond, Mrs. Mac tipped her face up and flashed blue eyes at her. "My dear, Ian says that your patient is a curly-headed young man handsome enough to melt any woman's heart."

Dora laughed. "Now don't you go getting any ideas. He's much too young for you. Besides, what would Doc say?"

Mrs. Mac smacked Dora's hands gently. "Ach, 'tis for you I'm thinking of him. And don't you go pretending you haven't noticed."

Dora grinned as she returned to dicing the vegetables. "Noticed what? That the edges of the abdominal wound are less reddened? The bruises on his face already fading? And the poor man is starving as we talk." She covered the stew and prepared a tray for the sickroom.

"Aye, that of course." Mrs. Mac turned so she could watch Dora's reactions. "And a whole lot more."

"The dumplings are ready to drop in. Wait about fifteen minutes," she called over her shoulder as she left the room balancing the tray.

Mrs. Mac called, "You got eyes in your head, girl. I know you do." The door clicked, shutting out anything more the older woman would have added.

Dora's grin faded. Certainly she'd noticed some of Josh's more appealing features. But she was no fool. She'd not be letting pretty curls or a handsome face cause her to make choices she'd regret.

Outside the sickroom, she paused to take a deep breath before she shoved open the door.

"That took awhile."

She nodded. "I made stew for Doc and his wife."

"Stew?" He perked up.

"And broth for you."

He groaned.

She pushed another pillow behind him and straightened the covers before setting a bed table across his chest to hold the tray.

He sniffed. "At least it smells like food." And he leaned forward eagerly as she fed him. He had just drained his cup of tea when Doc entered the room. Dora hurried to get a fresh dressing.

Doc lifted the bandage on Josh's forehead first. "Very good," he murmured then turned his attention to the lower wound. "Your injuries are healing well, young man."

"Does that mean I can get up soon?" Josh half pleaded.

"Now don't go undoing everything. You must wait awhile longer yet." Doc patted his shoulders. "You just lay still and enjoy the attention of a pretty young lass."

"I've been doing that, Doc."

Josh's gaze met Dora's. At his teasing

grin, heat flooded up her neck and she turned away.

Doc stood. "Josh, Dora's going home to get a good night's sleep, but I'll leave you with a cord that rings a bell in my living quarters. Should you have need of anything, just give it a yank." He turned to Dora. "I'll take the tray to the kitchen. You go on home now, lass."

Dora hesitated.

"Aw, Doc," Josh fussed. "You tell me to enjoy her company and then you send her home."

"I know, laddie. But she needs her rest." He shot a stern look in Dora's direction, but his voice was gentle as he said again, "You go on home. We'll see you in the morning."

She bid them both good night and left the office. As she stepped into her house, she knew Doc had been wise in sending her home. She was bone weary. She made a pot of tea, then sank into a big armchair and let her head fall back. Had only two days passed since Josh had been carried into the clinic half-alive? It seemed like she'd known him so much longer. Pushing to her feet, she decided she was more tired than hungry. She headed for bed, blaming her weariness for these thoughts that strayed down useless rabbit trails.

★ ★ ★

Doc was downing a cup of coffee when she hurried in the side door the next morning.

"Mrs. Mac is still sleeping. Josh is restless and bored. Do your best to keep him quiet." He took another swig of coffee. "He can have soft foods today." He was quiet for a moment. "And let him feed himself. All of his moving around yesterday appears to have done him no harm."

Dora met his flashing gaze. She should have known that they hadn't fooled him.

He set the cup down and grabbed his bag. "I'm off to visit Mrs. Smith. Have a good day." With no further ado, he was gone.

Humming, Dora quickly cleaned up Doc's breakfast and cooked some soft porridge for Josh. She set a place for Mrs. Mac, covering it with a clean towel. Still humming, she pushed open the sickroom door.

"I thought you'd never come back."

She smiled. "I've got your breakfast."

"I'm starving."

"Doc said you could have some real food today." She set up the bed table.

Josh looked at her suspiciously. "I'll bet."

"Really." She glanced at the tray as she set it before him. "Well almost. And Doc says you can feed yourself. Says you didn't do any damage yesterday with your moving about."

He grinned. "Wily old coyote." Without waiting for a response, he grabbed his spoon and, within minutes, polished off everything she'd prepared.

After she removed the tray, she set a basin of water before him. "Why don't you wash up a bit?"

Giving him some privacy, she took the dishes to the kitchen and plunged them into hot water. Her hands idly swirled the suds as she stared out the window, humming.

He was done when she returned and she tidied the room.

"How long before Doc lets me up?"

She could feel his barely-contained restlessness and hated to answer. "Probably ten days."

"Ten days." He closed his eyes.

"Perhaps he'll let you sit up in bed in two or three days."

He turned his tortured gaze toward her and whispered hoarsely, "I had hoped to be at my destination by now. Ten days! How can I delay that long?"

She bit her bottom lip. It was going to take a great deal of patience on his part to remain immobile as long as Doc wanted. She would do her best to help. Perhaps she could turn his attention to other things. "What made you take up the life of a cowboy?"

He took a deep breath and she knew he was trying valiantly to deal with his disappointment. "Horses, I guess. I wanted to be outside riding horses, not bent over machinery, never seeing the sun except on the way to and from the mill." He smiled and the tautness in her nerves unwound. "I wanted to see the sun cross the sky, breathe air off the damp soil, feel the wind in my face. I wanted the birds to be the song I heard while I worked, not the grind of millstones. I wanted to see the flowers as God created them, not the flour ground by man."

She laughed.

He continued. "Never mind God's goodness in providing the grain." He locked his fingers together under his head, his elbows wide, and grinned at her. "Guess that tells you more than you wanted to know."

Dora had stopped to watch the play of wonder and awe in his expression. Now she quickly bent her head and gave the basin another swipe with the towel. "Not at all." The way he talked made her yearn to see and feel things like he did, with open eagerness. He had accused her of thinking bad was good, which she did not. But neither did she embrace the beauties of life with such trust. She couldn't. She'd learned the hard way to plan her path, testing each step before she took it. She wanted to see where life was leading. She needed some control over the direction. Trusting God meant following carefully the way marked before her, not throwing oneself into riotous enjoyment without any regard for the future. No. That wasn't the way for her. She couldn't imagine it being the sensible way for anyone.

She was suddenly aware of his scrutiny and realized she had been quiet for several minutes. Gathering up her thoughts and containing them, she asked, "Didn't your folks mind?"

He nodded. "They minded me going. They didn't mind what I was doing."

"Tell me more about your family."

"We're big and noisy but I think we're a nice family. How about yours?"

Rather than answer, Dora asked, "You said something about a mill?"

"Yes. My dad and Uncle James own the mill at Morgan's Creek. It's a steady business but there's not enough income to support us all, even though Uncle James and Aunt Martha have no children." He shrugged. "That's why I was glad when Andy made it plain that he liked working in the mill. I didn't."

"I remember." She grinned. "You wanted to see the sky and taste the dust and smell the ground after a herd of cows had passed."

He laughed, then groaned and pressed his hands to his side. "You knew that would hurt, didn't you?"

She tightened her lips. "I didn't know you'd laugh." But she knew her eyes gave her away.

"Right. And I don't know what side of a horse to mount."

She could no longer hide the mirth bubbling inside her, so she turned away.

"Think it's funny, do you?"

She sobered and turned to face him. "Of course not." Laughing at someone's pain would be cruel. She would never do such a thing. But there was no stopping her wide smile.

An answering gleam shone from his eyes — eyes that held her own in a steady gaze. Her heart danced to a song in her head.

"You never did tell me about your family."

She blinked and pulled back, shaken by how quickly her thoughts had spun out of control. "No, I didn't." Pursing her lips, she turned away. Hands wringing, she sought some task to disguise her discomfort. The first thing she saw was the window. Three quick steps took her to stare out at the quiet street, her hands pleating and unpleating the curtains.

"Well?" Although quiet, his voice prodded her. She crushed the pleats in her hands then shrugged and turned.

"There's not much to tell." At least, not much she cared to tell. "There are four children. Two boys and two girls. I'm the oldest girl. My folks have a homestead twenty miles from town."

At the word homestead, Josh practically jerked upright. "What's it like? The homestead? How long has your father been there?"

Dora took a deep breath as the questions tumbled out of Josh's mouth. She had no desire to talk about it, but she guessed Josh would plague her now that he knew that much.

"They have a tough life." Dora intended to say no more. "I can't talk now. Doc will have my hide if I don't have the office and waiting room cleaned in time for his patients."

She crossed to the door then paused. She had briefly forgotten that Josh was also her patient. His care came before her own needs and desires. "Is there anything I can do for you before I go?"

Josh groaned behind her and Dora jerked around. Had he pulled something? But he stared up at the ceiling, his arms crossed over his chest. "I need to be out of here." He raised one hand in protest and grinned. "Don't say it. I already know. Lie quiet. Be patient." He groaned again. "I never realized how hard it is to do nothing." He made a shooing motion with his hand. "Go. I'll be all right."

Her duties called, but Dora hesitated to leave. She wanted to ease Josh's suffering during his stay. "Are you sure?" *I would love to talk with him all day — if only he wouldn't ask me any more questions about my family.*

He nodded.

She didn't hum as she tidied the rooms and prepared them for office hours. Instead, her thoughts circled round and round. It had been four years since she had escaped the homestead. Surely long enough to be able to think about the past without her insides getting brittle. Yet, just an innocent question or two turned her into a quivering mess. She pressed the heels of her hands into her eyes and moaned.

Grabbing the wet cloth, she scrubbed the examining table. Her pounding thoughts kept time with her frantic efforts. There had to be a way of putting aside her memories.

Prayer. That was the answer. She had prayed to be rescued from that situation, and God had wonderfully provided her with this chance. She would never cease to thank Him for it. Her thoughts slowed and she smiled. When Josh asked again about the homestead — and she was certain he would — she would tell him about life in town.

She glanced at the clock and gasped. *Lunch!* Rushing to the kitchen, she barely had time to prepare the chicken noodle soup that she had planned yesterday and take Josh a bowlful before Doc was calling her to the office. His first patients had arrived early.

They were rushed all afternoon. Then she hurried to make supper.

"You've had a busy day," Josh said as she carried in his tray. He waited as she set his meal on the table. "I heard an awful commotion one time."

"That was probably when Mrs. Baker came in with her brood of kids." Besides his Bible and the book he had yesterday, a child's storybook lay on the bed. Little Sam had left the book behind last winter after his recovery from pneumonia. She had planned to return it when she saw his family again. She laughed. "Found some good reading, did you?"

Josh grimaced. "It was the best I could do." He shook his head. "I'm so bored."

"And this helped?" She opened the pages.

" 'See Dick run. Run, Dick, run.' " He cradled one arm under his head and looked down his nose at her.

"It made a very interesting study."

"I'll bet." She chortled. "And exactly what did you learn from this 'interesting study'?"

He turned to face her, his eyes dark and unreadable. The laughter died in her throat. Her chest tightened. "I learned how boring recovery can be." His sigh lifted the bedcovers momentarily. Something ticked inside Dora's head, making it impossible for her to speak.

"Boring, boring, boring." Then he grinned. "But now that you're here I feel much better."

She blinked. It was nice to be appreciated. Josh made it seem even more special by his acknowledgment. "I'll find you some more mature books," she promised. "Unless you prefer this age level."

He grinned. "It's better than nothing. Almost."

"Doc has a collection of books and I have some as well. You are certainly welcome to borrow them."

Just then Doc entered and stared at the books on the bed. "I trust that you've been obeying orders, young man."

Josh held up his hands. "Best I can, Doc."

Doc waited until Josh finished his meal and Dora removed the tray before he checked the wounds. "You're doing fine." He stood. "Dora, ye go on home and remember tomorrow's the Sabbath. This young man will manage without nursing care tomorrow. If he needs anything, I'll see to it."

Dora had forgotten what day it was. She turned a startled gaze to Josh and caught the same protesting thought in his eyes. "But —"

"I mean it, Dora. Go home and enjoy a day of rest."

There was no arguing with Doc when he got that stubborn look on his face so she nodded. "I'll just get him a few of your books to read, if that's all right."

Doc nodded. "Aye. That will help him rest."

She ducked into the office and, skipping the medical texts, chose four adventure books. Doc had a fondness for tales of the north. She had skimmed through several and knew they were full of encounters with wild animals and accounts of fighting the elements, as well as equally unkind residents.

These were not the kind of stories she enjoyed, but perhaps Josh would. She delivered the books to his room.

Doc was still there, glowering. She hid a grin. Doc was determined to make sure that his orders were obeyed to the letter.

As she handed the books to Josh, he crooked his finger, indicating she should bend close. When she did, he barely whispered loud enough for her to hear. "Better hurry home. Doc looks like he'd as soon fry an egg on my forehead as have you miss your day of rest."

She choked back a chuckle and straightened slowly, giving herself time to compose her expression.

"I'll be going home now, Doc," she said in her sweetest, most compliant voice. "Say good night to Mrs. Mac for me."

Josh's chuckles followed Dora out of the room. Just before the door closed, she heard Doc growl, "Young whippersnapper." But she didn't know if his words were aimed at her or Josh.

Dora remained in the pew for several minutes following the service, her thoughts mulling over the points of the sermon. Pastor Luke Daley's favorite topics were faith, love, and forgiveness, and today he had chosen to preach about faith. As usual, his sermon was rich with illustrations and his message clear. Today, he had shown how one's choices in daily life revealed the depths of personal faith.

"It takes faith in God's provision," he had said, "to venture into the unknown."

Dora had agreed with him until he used homesteaders as an example of that type of faith. Perhaps, she conceded, for some folks, homesteading was a step of faith. Yet, others were drawn, not by faith, but by an illusion. Of this she was certain.

Dismissing her lingering thoughts, she joined the others as they filed out. Mary, Pastor Luke's wife and Dora's best friend, waited for her at the bottom of the steps.

"Stay until I've spoken to the rest, then we'll talk," Mary whispered as they hugged.

Dora nodded and stepped aside as Mary greeted each of the departing parishioners.

"You'll come for lunch, I hope," Mary said as she joined Dora.

"I was hoping you'd ask." It was a Sunday tradition for them. Even if Mary had invited others, as she often did, Dora was always included.

But today Dora was the only guest. They had barely sat down when Mary leaned toward Dora. "I hear you have a patient."

Dora nodded. "A cowboy who was hurt on the trail."

Mary lifted one eyebrow. "A young cowboy?"

Dora kept her face expressionless, knowing that Mary would read a hundred meanings into anything she imagined she saw. "A handsome, young man." Let her guess what that meant.

Mary's mouth made a perfect *O*.

Luke laughed. "She's setting you up, dearest," he warned.

Mary wrinkled her nose at him. "I know that. But I don't care." She turned back to Dora. "How young? How handsome?"

Dora pretended to give her questions a lot of thought. "Let's see." She pressed her finger to her lips. "He said he left home ten years ago. I guess that would make him at least twenty-six. Maybe a few years older."

Mary sighed and leaned back. "Just right for you."

"Why, I'm only twenty-two." Dora did her best to sound shocked.

Mary tsked. "Much too old to be without a husband. Or at least a beau."

"Indeed? Well, I have news for you. I'm quite happy without a man in my life. And much too busy to need one."

"Of course." But Dora knew Mary wasn't

agreeing. "And you admit he's handsome?"

"Oh yes." Dora closed her eyes, pretending to be overcome. "Dark curly hair and eyes as warm as —" She sighed rather than finish her sentence.

"Why I declare. I believe you're already half in love with him." Mary practically gloated.

Dora instantly grew serious. "Sorry to disappoint you, but he's headed west to get himself a homestead. Not my kind of man." And she took a mouthful of roast beef.

Luke laughed. "Told you, Mary."

"Some day she'll fall," Mary promised.

"I believe you're right, dearest," he said, turning to speak to Dora. "Someday I expect you'll make the astonishing discovery that some things are worth the risk-taking. Remember, security is not found in a place, or a position, or possessions, or even in security itself, but in God."

Stung by his assessment of her, Dora stared at him. "Do you really think I'm trusting in something other than God?"

Mary rushed to her defense. "I'm sure he didn't mean that, did you dear?"

"No, of course I didn't. I've seen your faith. But I believe God stretches us all lest we grow complacent." He pushed his chair back. "Now if you girls will excuse me, I am going to my office."

After he left, the two young women were quiet a moment.

"I'm sure he didn't mean to criticize you, Dora." Mary kept her face toward her plate.

Dora touched her friend's arm. "I don't feel like he was." But a shiver flickered across her neck. He had warned of change and she didn't welcome the thought.

Determined to lighten the mood, she asked, "Are you looking forward to the concert?" She spoke of the traveling singing group scheduled to appear next week.

Mary wriggled in her seat. "With great expectation. I can hardly wait. I hear that this is the best group we've had yet."

"You've managed to get some good entertainment." Mary belonged to a committee that arranged a special concert three or four times a year. "After that there's the church picnic, then the debating team."

"Don't forget the ball tournament."

Dora nodded. She enjoyed the crowd and visiting much more than the sport, but Luke was an ardent ball player so Mary counted ball tournaments high on the list of activities.

Later, at home in her tiny rooms, Dora thought about the day. Let Pastor Luke make his dire predictions; she knew better.

It wasn't lack of faith that made her determined to enjoy what God had provided. After all, hadn't she proven her faith when she left home with nothing more than a worn satchel containing a second dress? She had prayed fervently for God to help her find a place to stay, and He had miraculously provided. He made it possible for her to finish her schooling by working after classes in return for her board. And, incredibly, a job in the hotel had opened up for her right after graduation. The job was not one she liked, but again she had prayed and trusted God. Now He had given her this job with Doc Mackenzie. And she loved her job. Perhaps, someday, she would enter formal nurse's training and improve her skills.

All the talk of Josh had triggered Luke's comments. He and Mary were always nagging her about finding a fellow and getting married.

But, she vowed, she would never allow herself to fall in love with someone like Josh.

She prepared for bed early, anxious for the morrow when she could return to work.

The checkerboard lay across Josh's bed. Dora put the checker pieces in place. "I'm going to beat you this time for sure."

Josh lay back, his arms under his head.

"You probably could if you paid attention."

"Paid attention, indeed."

"I'll even let you go first."

She narrowed her eyes and studied him. Did letting her go first give him an advantage? Ducking her head to study the board, she admitted she didn't understand strategy. What difference did it make which checker she moved first? Oh, she hated to see him win so easily. Finally she moved a checker.

"Did I ever tell you about the time a grizzly bear licked my boots?" His attention was riveted on the game board, so she couldn't see his eyes. "Your turn."

She hesitated then moved again. "Is this another of your tall tales?"

His hand to his chest, he drew back. "I swear I didn't make up any of them. Though I couldn't guarantee the same for my friend, Twister. He insisted that he got his name from riding a corkscrew mustang. But I always kinda figgered it was because of the way he twisted the truth. Your turn."

Dora's hand hovered over the game pieces then she jumped one of his checkers and set it on the edge of the board.

"Anyway, we were taking a break from branding and I wandered down by the river. The day was nice and sunny, so I sat down by a log and closed my eyes. Your turn.

"All of a sudden, I felt this bump against my foot. I opened my eyes and there was a grizzly licking my boots. It's your turn again."

Dora squinted at the board. How did he make his plays so fast? She hadn't even followed what he'd done. She reached for one checker but caught herself before she touched it. Moving that one would set up a chain of jumps. She chose a different one.

"It was just a cub, maybe two or three hundred pounds.

"Well, you can bet I figured I was bear breakfast. I gave a quick look around for the momma and saw her about two hundred yards away with a second cub. They were rooting at an old tree stump. Probably eating bugs." He jumped his man across the board and set three of her game buttons on the side. "Your turn.

"I eased away from the cub and, slow as I could, got to my feet. You understand, now I was in a big hurry to leave, but I didn't want to set the cub to crying. All the same, the cub woofed. Old momma bear rose up on her hind feet. Your turn."

His checkers were all over the board, but if she moved one of hers against the edge . . .

"I high-tailed it out of there. I could hear

that momma bear thudding at my heels. I raced toward the camp." He paused. "Your turn again."

"Josh. For goodness' sake, tell me what happened." She gave the board a quick glance and saw an opening.

"I got ate up."

"Yeah. And came out the other end almost normal."

His smirk changed to a frown, then he laughed. "I guess not. No, I ran and ran. As soon as I saw the men gathered around the fire, I started hollering, 'Bear. Bear.' They just stood there gaping at me. I skidded around the cook wagon, wheezing fit to kill. As soon as I could, I looked behind me. And there was nothing." He shrugged. "Guess what I thought was the bear chasing me was really my own heart thudding." He jumped three more of her checkers. "Crown me."

She was staring at Josh, caught in his bear story. She closed her mouth and gave Josh his crowning checker, then moved one of her own men.

"I never did quite live it down. Every so often, when things got boring, one of the men would get all big-eyed and flap his arms in my face and yell, 'Bear.' " He shrugged. "It was kind of funny."

Dora began to chuckle. "I can just see

you." She nodded — "Bear. Bear." — and laughed harder. "Wish I could have been there."

"Yeah, well, it might not have turned out so good." He crossed his arms over his chest. "By the way, I beat you again."

Sobering instantly, she studied the board and saw he was right. "It's not fair. You distracted me."

He shrugged. "Wasn't much of a challenge."

"Why you!" She flung a handful of checkers at him.

He flipped them away, except for one that he flicked back at her.

She ducked, laughing. "Stop now. You're supposed to be resting."

His deep chuckles made her laugh harder and just about the time she had it under control, their eyes met and she started again. She couldn't remember when she'd had this much fun.

Chapter 3

Over the next few days Dora and Josh spent a great deal of time together as she tried to help him while away the hours. They talked about books they'd read, things they enjoyed, and Josh told her more about his family.

She did what she could to make his convalescence pleasant and, in so doing, grew to enjoy his company more and more. He was a good patient, striving to be cheerful and cooperative even when she knew he ached to head west.

Five days later Doc bent over Josh's dressing. "Young man, you have done very well." He wiped his hands on a towel. "How would ye feel about getting up for a wee while this morning?"

Josh's eyes grew wide, then narrowed suspiciously. "You wouldn't be pulling my leg now, would you, Doc?"

Doc beckoned to Dora. "You take one side, lass, and I'll be holding the other." He flipped the covers back and eased Josh's legs over the side of the bed. Dora helped him to sit and steadied him as he swayed.

"Not to worry, son. You'll be a bit shaky at first." Doc kept his fingers on Josh's wrist, checking his pulse. "Sit until the dizziness passes and then we'll try standing."

Josh hung his head and groaned.

"Take a deep breath and let it out slowly," Dora instructed.

"Ready?" Doc asked after a moment.

Josh nodded and together they stood. He swayed, his weight pressing against Dora. She watched his face, saw the color slip away and return as he gritted his teeth and steadied himself.

"I'm all right," he grunted.

Dora glanced at Doc. He nodded slightly.

"Let's try a step or two." They shuffled forward as a unit and stopped. "Turn now, lad," Doc said.

With Doc and Dora on each side, he turned and shuffled back to the bed where he collapsed, sweat beading his brow.

"That was fine, laddie. Just fine." Doc checked Josh's pulse and lifted his legs to the bed. "Now you rest a bit and we'll get you up again later. Dora, get the boy some lunch."

By suppertime, Doc announced that Josh could join them in the kitchen if he felt well enough.

"I'll do it," he eagerly replied. He had insisted on donning his clothes earlier in the afternoon and now he jerked to his feet.

Dora tightened her lips as Josh, holding himself stiff and upright, walked down the hall to the kitchen.

The next day Doc suggested that Josh might like to sit outside on the verandah and enjoy the warm sunshine. "You'll soon be well enough to be on your way, lad."

Doc's words thumped into the pit of Dora's stomach. Her hands froze in mid-air.

"I'm glad to hear that." Josh sounded a great distance away.

She took a steadying breath. Had she caught a hesitant note in his voice? She darted a glance at him. A mix of emotions flashed through his expression. She was sure his eagerness was tainted by something sad. Well, what should she expect? He'd never faltered in wishing he could be on his way.

Nevertheless, Dora would be sorry to see him go. He had been a good patient and she enjoyed his company.

Before Doc could scold her for dilly-dallying, she hurried outside and moved the wicker rocker into the sun. Josh came out with Doc at his heels. Dora waited until

Josh settled into a comfortable position, then she followed Doc inside.

"There's a lad who's through and through nice," Doc said as he folded his stethoscope into his bag and prepared to leave. "You'd do well to have a closer look at him, lassie."

"I —" But not waiting for her reply, Doc grabbed his hat and headed for the door.

Dora stared after him. What a strange comment from Doc. He knew better than anyone how hard she had worked to be where she was.

Pausing on the threshold, Doc glanced over his shoulder at her. "Be sure, lassie, that you don't overlook a prize when you find it." Then, before she could answer, he was gone.

She put the instruments to boil, tidied Doc's desk, and swept the waiting room floor. All the while, her thoughts circled round Doc's comments like a buzzard after a bone.

She would miss Josh something fierce. He had proven himself amusing and entertaining. But his plans hadn't changed. He was headed west to try his hand at farming.

Dora's plans had not altered either. She intended to enjoy what God had provided right here in Freebank.

Her chores done, she checked out the

window. Josh sat with his feet up on the rail and a book in his lap, but his gaze on some distant spot.

A pair of girls passed — Jenny, the storekeeper's daughter, and another she didn't recognize. Jenny's eyes widened as she spied Josh and she nudged her friend. The two giggled, then Jenny called, "Hello, sir. I trust you are enjoying the sunshine."

Josh slowly lowered his gaze and smiled at the passing pair. "Good morning, ladies. It's a fine day." He seemed oblivious to their adoration and returned to his contemplation of the far horizon.

They hesitated then sauntered past, preening and smiling.

Dora smiled. If they thought to engage him in a flirtation, they had failed. Feeling rather pleased, she headed to the kitchen to make coffee and start lunch. That done, she prepared a tray for Josh and marched down the hall toward the verandah.

At the sound of her footsteps, he looked up, his eyes dark with welcome.

A shock shot through her as her heart responded to his look.

She almost dropped the tray. The rope handles ground into her palm. The coffee scent stung her nose. The bright air was filled with birds' song and the happy sound of children at play. Her heart leapt for the dazzling sky and she nearly stumbled.

He attempted to rise as she stepped outside.

"Stay where you are," she ordered, her insides wobbling as she set the tray on the railing. "I thought you might like some coffee."

"You read my mind."

Keeping her face averted, she poured him a cup and offered him a cookie, all the while trying to ignore her tempestuous emotions.

"Aren't you going to join me?"

His words jolted across her nerves and she jerked to attention. "I have work to do," she muttered. Without so much as a backward glance, Dora raced inside.

Pressing her palms to her tight chest, she leaned against the door waiting for her panic to subside.

She'd promised herself that she would not let this happen. Josh was set on heading west, and she could not — would not — venture into the way of life he had chosen.

She would not allow herself to love such a man. Yet her pulse throbbed at the mere thought of him.

How could she have fallen in love with him? She wanted to cry and shake her hands in his face. Instead, she moaned.

I do not love him. I will not love him. We are headed in opposite directions. All I have to do is keep my distance for a few more days. Doc will surely discharge him and I can forget I ever met him. Nodding briskly in agreement with her renewed resolve, she hurried off to the kitchen to prepare the evening meal.

Josh came in a short time later and looked around the kitchen.

"Where's Mrs. Mac? I thought I'd keep her company until supper is ready."

She must have heard his voice, for Mrs. Mac scurried in from the front room, her cheeks flushed like she'd been dozing.

"Ah, Mrs. Mac, I was hoping to see you." He plucked two cups from the cupboard and poured coffee. "I want to hear all about your trip from the Old Country." He ushered her into the front room. Dora heard a chair being moved and knew he was making sure Mrs. Mac was comfortable.

Dora smiled. It hadn't taken him long to discover that the doctor's wife loved to talk about the Old Country and her family back there. Their voices rocked back and forth, one deep and strong, the other soft and reedy.

She tried not to feel annoyance at Josh's preference for Mrs. Mac's company over her own. She gave her head a flick. Things were better this way. The less time she spent with him, the easier it would be to forget him when he left.

Doc returned and the four of them sat down for their evening meal. Dora jumped up every few minutes to get something from the stove or pantry. If Mrs. Mac wondered why Dora felt an urgency to have jam on the table during supper, she didn't mention it. However, Doc raised his eyebrows when Dora got a second gravy boat and transferred the gravy from one container to the other.

The minute Doc set his fork down, Dora scooped up his plate and started washing dishes.

"Seems we aren't going to linger tonight," Doc commented, his voice dry. "Dora seems anxious to get the place cleaned up."

She felt three pairs of questioning eyes on her but kept her back turned and her hands immersed in soapy water. She hadn't meant to rush them. But she felt a sudden, desperate need to get to her own rooms where she could sort out her thoughts.

"I think I'll run along." She swiped the table. "That is, if I'm not needed for anything more." She hung the towel and wet rag over the towel bar.

"I expect we can manage without you."

At Doc's teasing tone, she glanced up and caught him winking at his wife.

A small frown furrowed Mrs. Mac's brow before she turned and smiled at Dora. "Yes, dear, you go on home. You've worked hard all week."

Josh tipped his chair back. "I can certainly take care of myself. Have for years."

Dora lowered her head. She knew she was behaving strangely, but she couldn't stop her insides from twisting and turning. Even so, she knew she had no excuse. She took a steadying breath and looked up. "I'm sorry. I didn't mean to be impolite. I just suddenly realized how much I have to do at home." She let her gaze touch each of them then turned and prepared to leave.

Doc harumphed.

"It's quite all right, dear," Mrs. Mac said. "We do understand."

"You have a good night, Dora." Josh's voice, so filled with kindness, was almost her undoing. Nodding, she hurried out.

By the time she closed the door of her house she was gasping for breath. She leaned against the wall of the dark room and waited for the pounding in her head to ease. Slowly she relaxed and gained control of her thoughts.

She had gone and done what she promised herself she would *not* do. She had fallen in love with Josh. How foolish to let this bother her so! Josh need never know how he had affected her. He would leave town in a few days, and she would soon forget all about him. In the meantime, she must still serve as his nurse — though there was little she needed to do anymore. She simply had to act normal.

Having thus consoled herself, she prepared for bed.

She overslept the next morning and had to hurry to get ready for church. She was about ready to walk out the door when a knock sounded on the other side. Dora drew her hand to her chest in alarm. Her heart thudding, she pulled open the door.

"Hi," Josh greeted her, his face swathed in a smile. "Doc said it would do me good to go to church. He seemed pretty sure you'd be willing to show me the way."

Dora snorted. The old codger was determined to get the two of them interested in each other. She wondered what he would say if he knew that he didn't have to try on her behalf.

"Certainly," she said to Josh. "You're more than welcome to come with me." Her insides as unsteady as a newborn calf, she faced the room, foolishly relishing every minute spent with him. How could she bear the bittersweet moments of his company while still keeping her secret? And what on earth was Mary going to say?

Filling her lungs and ordering her insides to be quiet, she demurely announced, "I'm ready."

He stepped aside to let her pass, then fell into step beside her as they walked the four blocks to church.

"It's a fine morning, is it not?"

Dora's stomach fluttered at the sound of his voice.

"Why, I can hear a half-dozen different birds singing in the trees as we pass. Listen. Can you catch the robin's song?"

She cocked her head as though to listen, then nodded in agreement. But she hadn't heard the robin's song. The music she heard was the music of her own heart. Dora let the sweet melody swirl through her until she thought she could contain it no longer. Closing her eyes, she took a deep breath.

I must stop. My heart is running away from my head. He'll soon be gone.

She blinked, struggling to settle her emotions. Then a wayward thought surfaced. *All the more reason to enjoy every precious moment we have left to share.*

They'd come to the corner and he grasped her elbow, gently guiding her across the street.

Her nerves tightened until she feared her heart would burst. She forced herself to stare straight ahead. Surely his behavior was as always, and it was her heightened awareness of him that now made his every word and every touch reverberate with shock waves.

"I hope you don't think I'm presumptuous." He let her arm go as they reached the other side of the street. Suddenly, her legs went weak. To cover her confusion, she paused to smooth her skirt.

"I ordered a picnic lunch," he said. "I was hoping you'd share it with me in the park after the service."

"Why I'd like that very much." Her throat tightened so that her words squeaked. Thankfully they met several others on their way to church and a round of greetings and introductions gave Dora's breathing a chance to slow.

Her senses remained razor-sharp throughout the service. The singing seemed richer and fuller than she remembered as Josh's deep voice blended with hers. The light coming through the windows seemed to have a white quality about it, cleansing those in its path.

Luke spoke of love and every word dripped honey into Dora's heart.

Afterwards, wrapped in a glow, Dora filed down the aisle until she stood before Mary and Luke.

"I'd like you to meet Josh Rivers." She tried to ignore Mary's pleased expression as she made the introductions.

When Mary hugged her, Dora whispered in her ear, "I've agreed to have lunch with Josh. I hope you don't mind."

Mary snorted. "Mind. I guess not. I'm glad you've decided to open your eyes."

"It's not that way." But she knew her protests were wasted as Mary patted her cheek and nodded.

"Dora, I've got eyes, too, and I know what I see."

Dora gave up and said good-bye.

They walked to the hotel where Josh picked up the picnic lunch he had ordered. Then, they sauntered to the center of town to the park burgeoning with spring.

"The young preacher delivered a good sermon." Josh spread a blanket on the grass and opened the basket.

"He's a good man." She helped set out the jug of lemonade and glasses. "We're blessed to have him."

Josh passed the plate of sandwiches to her and she chose egg salad. He chose one with roast beef and leaned his back against a tree. "This seems a real nice little town."

"I think it is. We have all the essentials — school, church, stores — plus lots of nice extras." She went on to tell about the social activities.

"This park is really beautiful." She followed his glance from the little footbridge to the gazebo nestled in the trees and to the winding path along the lake.

"It began as someone's yard. A lady from England. She loved flowers and gardens. Many of the flower gardens were made by her." She pointed out the ones she was certain had been original. "Her husband built the footbridge. When she died, she left the land to the town with the stipulation that it be used as a park." Josh nodded, his eyes warm with interest.

Her tongue grew thick at the look on his face and she ducked her head to finish her story. "That was Mrs. Free. The town was built on a piece of her husband's land. Hence the name, Freebank."

"Gives the town a right nice feel. I can see why you like this place so much."

He didn't know the half of it. And she couldn't tell him.

Neither of them spoke. Around them filtered the sounds of other people in the park, accompanied by the swelling songs of birds rejoicing in spring and love and building new nests.

Josh cleared his throat and Dora jerked her gaze to him.

He watched her with a keenness that sent her heart into flight.

"Doc says I'll be able to go in a few more days."

She nodded, her mouth suddenly dry. She knew this moment would come. Perhaps it was best to come sooner rather than later — before her heart led her where she could not go. Nevertheless, her insides plummeted like a rock.

"I need to get going."

Again she nodded, well aware of how much work faced him.

He pushed away from his backrest and leaned toward her. He was so close, she could have touched his face with her trembling fingertips. She squeezed her hands into a tight ball and buried them in her lap.

"Dora." His voice was low and intense. "I haven't known you very long but it's long enough for me to realize that — er." Josh stumbled on his words. "I–I . . . well, I can't imagine never seeing you again."

Her heart pounded in her throat as, dumbstruck, she stared at him.

"Dora, I've fallen madly and completely in love with you. Just seeing your face and hearing your voice makes my heart sing like these spring-crazed birds around us."

Every word dropped like gentle rain into her heart, adding to the emotion that she had been collecting there — emotion that now threatened to overflow the barriers she had erected.

"Dora, I'm asking you to marry me and go with me to the foothills. We'll find the prettiest spot in all the world and build our own little home, filled with love and laughter."

His words were a song of love — the sweetest sound she'd ever heard. And she almost succumbed. Almost. Then she forced herself to remember the years she'd spent on the farm with her parents. Homesteading held no allure for her. She knew all too well what it meant.

She would never again make herself endure such suffering and hardship.

"Josh, I'm flattered." She avoided his gaze. "But I can't."

She heard him sharply inhale a breath and hated herself for hurting him.

"I guess I read you wrong." His voice

sounded strained. "I thought you might care about me."

Her heart shredded. "You weren't wrong," she whispered. "I do care about you." She swallowed hard. "I love you."

His smile flashed and he leaned forward eagerly.

But she turned away. "But I would never go homesteading."

He jerked back like she'd slapped him. "Why not?"

Stung by his reaction, she faced him. "I spent two years of sheer torture living without enough of anything and never having one bit of luxury or enjoyment. Homesteading meant nothing but work and depravation, and I vowed I would never do it again."

The light fled from his eyes and for a moment she wished she could change her mind. But remembering those years, she stiffened.

"I literally thought I would die." Every nerve in her body ached just remembering. "My dad knew nothing of farming. He made every mistake in the book. We ran out of food the first winter and had to accept charity from some neighbors. My dad and brother built a house, but there wasn't enough money for more than the shell.

Snow came through the cracks. I woke up more than once with my toes numb from cold." She choked back tears. "I didn't get warm all winter." Suddenly she couldn't stop. "I outgrew my clothes and had to wear some of my grandmother's old dresses, which made me feel dirt-ugly. Day in and day out, we did nothing but work. There was no church, no school, no nothing." She caught her breath. "I didn't know if we'd starve to death or freeze or simply die of exhaustion." Her voice dropped to a whisper. "I'll never go through such torture again."

Josh stared at her, his eyes round. She turned away not wanting his pity.

"Oh, Dora, it sounds all horns and rattles. I'm sorry it was so bad." He paused. "But homesteading isn't always that way. I've talked to many—"

"I've heard plenty of lies, too," she hissed. "But I've been there. I know."

He nodded. "How are your folks now?"

"They were fine when I saw them at Christmas." She found it impossible to understand how the rest of her family could now be so content. She wouldn't attempt to offer Josh an explanation.

"Are things any better for them?"

"I suppose." The inside of the house had been finished, the oilcloth placed on the floors, and Mother had been given a new dress. Father talked about spring like it held all the diamonds in the world.

She felt, rather than saw, Josh nod. "They believed the dream and set out to realize it."

She flung around to face him. "What dream? More like a nightmare, if you ask me." She swept her gaze over the park. "A dream would be beautiful like this — full of pleasure and enjoyment. Not pinched, barely-alive torture."

He shrugged and held out his hands in surrender. "I can see you aren't prepared to look at this any other way."

"What other way is there?"

"There's sacrifice in order to achieve a goal. You said your father wasn't a farmer, yet many people have learned because they're willing to learn. That's what I meant when I asked how things are now. Did your father learn how to farm? Did your family have faith? Do they still?"

"Faith?" She fairly spit the word out. "Faith is believing in what God promises, not what the government promises. Faith is using the good sense God gives us, not jumping in front of a train and expecting God to rescue us."

"You're right as far as you go — but faith also includes venturing into the unknown and believing, even when we can't see the end result."

She shook her head. "I guess you can use words any way you want, but it all boils down to one thing. It's madness to try and build something out of nothing."

"Ah, but there's where you're wrong. It isn't, as you say, 'nothing.' God has provided the best land in the world, practically free. And I know about cattle and farming. I know how to make something out of the bounty God has offered."

She frowned. "What about grasshoppers, hail, frost? What about sickness? What about all the things over which you have no control?"

He smiled sadly. "None of us can control the future whether we live in town or on a homestead. That's where faith comes in. If you think you can guarantee a safe and predictable future by living in town and refusing to accept love or take risks, then I fear you are in for a dry-bones existence or a very harsh disappointment. Trusting God means leaving the future in His hands."

Rather than answer, Dora gathered up the leftover sandwiches and the untouched cake and returned them to the basket. Josh flung the blanket over his shoulder and scooped up the basket, waiting for Dora to draw abreast. Silently, they headed home, their steps quicker and more determined than they had been earlier. As they crossed Main Street, Josh drew in a sharp breath and ducked down a lane.

Dora stared after him. He hurried to the shadow of a wood shed and pulled close to the building.

"Josh?" She squinted, trying to see his face in the gloom.

"Shush."

Hesitating, she tried to decide if she should follow or wait. Finally deciding it would be best to join him, she turned into the alley. At the same time, he reappeared from the building's shadows and stepped into the sunlight, his eyes searching behind her. "I'm dead certain that was Slim and Chester."

She wrinkled her brow. "Who?"

"The varmints who stole my money and left me half-dead." His eyes darkened and he frowned. "Bet they'd be surprised to see me."

Dora gaped at him.

"In fact, I might just jump out of the shadows and scare the dickens out of them."

Her heart did a strange little flip-flop and her throat seemed suddenly too tight. "Do you suppose they're looking for you?" She had visions of them hunting Josh down and finishing what they'd begun almost two weeks ago.

"I'm guessing they think I'm dead."

A shudder raced up her spine. Josh's steps halted and she was surprised to see that they were in front of her house. Her glance jerked from her front door to Josh's face and then past his shoulder. When she saw no approaching figures, she turned her concentration to Josh and what he was saying.

"I wish you'd give my offer more thought. The future is not as frightening as you think — especially when you share it with someone you love."

She shook her head. The present was suddenly frightening enough. Never mind the future. But her anger had disappeared and she regretted saying all those things. "Josh, I really do love you. But I cannot possibly become a homesteader's wife. I'm sorry." Unable to bear the pain in his eyes, she fled indoors.

Chapter 4

Dora peered out from her bedcovers into the darkness and prayed for strength.

She knew what was right for her, but as she reflected on her conversation with Josh, her choices seemed childish and fearful. Hadn't God given her this place and this job? She wasn't about to toss these blessings back in His face.

In time Josh would forget her.

She tossed about seeking a comfortable position, trying desperately to avoid the truth.

She would never forget him. Not if she lived to be a hundred years old. She tried in vain to ignore the ache in her heart.

Abandoning the hope of sleep, she waited for morning and the moment that she could hurry across the street. Even as her pulse raced at the thought, she wondered how she would face him.

The next morning, she hesitated before she opened the door and entered Doc's house. Doc greeted Dora by saying, "Our young man is out."

"Josh?"

"Aye, Josh. He was dressed and waiting when I got up. Said he was going for a ride. Time to test his strength, he said." Doc shook his head. "Seemed mighty troubled about something in my opinion." He studied Dora with questioning eyes.

In no mood to match wits with Doc, she turned and hastened across the room to fling open the door to the bedroom. The bed was tossed, but Josh and his clothes were missing. She swallowed hard.

Perhaps it was for the best. Then she saw his saddlebags hooked on the post, his books, and the picture of his family lying on the shelf. Relief flooded her.

Doc had followed her and she said to him, "He must have gone for a ride like you said. See, he's left his things."

"Well, I didn't think he'd leave without saying good-bye," Doc gruffly replied. "I must be on my way."

She nodded. "And I have much to do."

But all the time she cleaned and dusted and prepared meals and helped Doc with patients, her ears were tuned to catch the sound of a horse riding into the yard or boots crossing the verandah.

The day ended without hearing the

sounds she strained to catch and she returned home without seeing him.

Her nerves tight as fence wire under a heavy frost, she paced her rooms for an hour then, unable to endure the strain any longer, she grabbed a sweater and hurried out the door. Perhaps a visit to Mary would ease her mind.

At the parsonage, Mary drew Dora quickly inside. "I've been longing for some company. Luke's at the church."

Dora hid her relief at the news. Sometimes Luke seemed to see through her with startling clarity. He was often right, a fact which, she admitted wryly, did nothing to make her more comfortable. Smiling at Mary's eagerness, she allowed herself to be led into the kitchen. She could always talk freely with Mary.

"What brings you here so early in the week? I thought you'd be taking a stroll in the park with that handsome young man of yours."

"He's not mine."

"Girl, you must be blind. I saw the way his eyes followed you. If that young man isn't head over heels in love, then I'm–I'm an old fat hen."

Dora grinned, and putting her hands in her armpits, she strutted around the room. "Cluck, cluck," she said, flapping her elbows.

Mary scowled. "You don't fool me. I saw the two of you together." She waited for Dora to return to her chair. "So what's the problem?"

Tossing her head, Dora asked, "Who says there's a problem?"

"Fine. Pretend you didn't come to see me because something's troubling you. We'll simply have ourselves a nice cup of tea." She filled the pot as she spoke. "And we'll talk about something else." She brought the pot to the table and set out two cups. "Did you see the new outfit Mrs. Mellon had on? Where does she get her clothes? There's nothing like that in town, and I certainly didn't see anything that special in the Eaton's catalogue. I think it was real fur on the collar of her dress." Mary closed her eyes for a moment. "Don't you think I'd look lovely in such a nice outfit?"

She poured the tea and hurried on. "And where was Abigail? She hasn't been to church for three weeks now. Have you heard if she's ill or away?" She hesitated barely long enough to catch her breath. "No? Well, I was just wondering. And how's Mrs. Mac? She's such a nice lady. I hope she gets stronger now that spring is here. I shudder to think of Doc taking her away. What would we do without him?"

Dora scowled at her friend, annoyed at her silly chatter. She'd come to tell her problems, not listen to a recital of what everyone else said or wore. Mary should know better.

Then, again, Mary had offered to listen, but she had refused. As Mary's incessant prattle continued, Dora felt a chuckle rising from within. Finally, she could contain her laughter no longer. "Enough. Of course I came here to talk. You don't have to make a production out of it."

Mary grinned and leaned back. "So what's the problem?"

"Josh."

"No." Mary pretended shock, covering her mouth with her hand.

Dora shook her head sadly. "I'm afraid so." Suddenly all the silliness was gone. "I love him."

Mary nodded.

"He says he loves me."

Mary clapped her hands. "Lovely."

Dora shook her head again. "Not lovely. He wants me to marry him and go with him to stake out a homestead in the Wild West."

"Yes?" Mary waved her hands impatiently.

"That's just it. I can't go west with him."

"Why ever not?"

"I'm as far west as I plan to go."

Mary shook her head. "I don't understand."

Dora stared at her. "He's a cowboy with a head full of dreams and pockets full of dust. And a gilded tongue to boot. But you, of all people, should know why I can't go."

Her eyes narrowing, Mary studied Dora. "Are you referring to the life you lived out on the farm before you came to town?"

Dora's lips tightened. "I could never live like that again. I won't have people feeling sorry for me."

Mary jerked back. "Sorry? Who feels sorry for you? Or your family? As far as I know, your father is a respected man. He's worked hard and has every right to be proud. What makes you say that?"

Dora shrugged. "It's just that life is so uncertain. Sometimes you get a crop and have money. Other times you don't know how you'll survive. And life is so barren."

Mary smiled. "Enjoyment is a state of mind."

"What's that supposed to mean?"

"Don't you realize that even the most mundane things become events if your heart is happy and whole?"

"It's hard to be happy when life is so uncertain." Dora shook her head unable to fathom how Mary could be so obtuse when she was generally so agreeable.

Mary continued. "I don't understand. A preacher's life is uncertain. We'll never have much. Some days we don't have enough for the next week. Some would say we depend on other people for our survival. Of course, we don't. We depend on God." She drew herself up stiffly. "Do you feel sorry for us?"

Dora sighed. "Of course not. But you're so happy, why would anyone feel sorry for you?"

Mary nodded. "That's it exactly. We're happy anyway. Our circumstances don't dictate how we feel."

Miserable, Dora studied her fingernails. How could she explain how she felt when her emotions were a tangle of fear and reluctance and resolve? She had vowed never to make the kind of mistakes her parents had made — risking everything for a bit of land; facing disaster, failure, and hunger for the right to own one miserable quarter section.

As Dora prepared to leave, Mary looked troubled. "I fear you are clutching too hard to a security that is an illusion. Who can say that life in town will always be so pleasant? Besides, it is always a meaningless sacrifice to forego love and cling to shallow substitutes."

Dora frowned. It was easy for Mary to talk. From the time she'd seen Luke she'd known what she wanted.

Mary, having read her expression, hugged her arm. "I don't mean to give you pat answers. I'll pray God will guide your steps."

Dora hurried home. As she rounded the last corner, she strained to catch a glimpse of light coming from the window of Josh's room. Only blackness greeted her. Dora's steps faltered. Even though she had refused his offer, she hadn't expected him to simply disappear.

With heavy feet, she climbed the steps to her house.

The next morning she entered Doc's house as he rushed out. "Our young man has not returned." Doc shook his head. "I don't understand these modern young people."

Dora watched him hurry down the steps, then turned her attention to the day's work. She spent a few minutes in Josh's room straightening the bed and rearranging the articles. She barely had time to clean the office before there was a burst of activity. The day was busy with a rash of broken bones and some minor injuries from children recklessly enjoying the freedom of spring.

But despite the busyness, the tightness around Dora's heart intensified with each passing hour. She hurried from the last patient to the kitchen and began supper, cooking a large pot of potatoes and frying an extra steak all the while refusing to admit that she expected Josh to walk in at any moment.

Mrs. Mac came into the kitchen. "Where is Josh? I haven't seen him all day."

Her voice echoed the impatience of Dora's heart. Poor Mrs. Mac. Josh had brought a ray of sunshine to her life. Now he was gone. Disguising her own disappointment and concern, she answered gently, "He told Doc he was going for a ride. I expect he'll be back soon."

"That was yesterday. He should have been back long ago." She perched on the edge of her chair. "Something must have happened to the poor boy. I know it."

Dora grabbed the back of a chair as pain shot through her. Could he be injured? "Not again," she whispered, remembering his condition such a short while ago.

"Did you say something, lassie?"

"I was only thinking aloud."

"Care to share your thoughts with an old lady?" Mrs. Mac waggled her eyebrows.

Dora smiled. "I don't think you would

want to hear my muddled thoughts."

Mrs. Mac snorted, and Dora knew she was waiting for her to say more, but she turned the steaks again and checked the pots without adding to her comment.

Doc came into the room and pulled out a chair. They were all waiting for Josh's appearance.

Finally, Doc sighed loudly. "I expect we might as well go ahead without him."

The three of them had little to say as Dora dished up the food.

"Perhaps he's decided he feels well enough to continue his journey," Doc said. "Though I would have thought he would say farewell." He paused then added, "I suppose he will write when he settles and have us send his things."

Doc's words echoed as Dora returned to her house to prepare for choir practice. Josh had left without saying good-bye. It hurt, even though she realized it was for the best.

Choir was one of her greatest pleasures. She loved music and she found tremendous enjoyment in blending her voice with the others. At least she had until tonight, she thought after she missed another note.

One of the young married women asked the group to her home for refreshments following practice, and Dora agreed despite the ache inside. After all, she reasoned, wasn't social activity one of the reasons she insisted she had to live in town? But the chatter and noise made her head ache, and she slipped away early, pleading tiredness. She returned to her home to spend another troubled night.

The next morning, she stepped into Doc's kitchen and blinked. Mrs. Mac was up and dressed, eating toast with her husband.

"Did you notice the Mayday tree?" she asked happily. "It's in blossom."

Dora stopped in her tracks. It had become a tradition to measure the seasons by the trees and flowers. The Mayday tree was their spring marker. When the tree blossomed with its fragrant white flowers, they all agreed, spring had officially arrived. Dora had watched for days, hoping to be the first to spot the blooms. She thought she had an advantage, for she passed the tree each morning. But she had walked by this morning without seeing the tree or even noticing the scent. She shook her head. She must have been half-asleep.

The day, although busy, passed slowly. Dora tried to tell herself that she had accepted Josh's leaving. But as she rubbed her aching brow she wished she could convince her heart.

By evening she wanted nothing but to crawl into bed and cover up her head. Still, her thoughts kept sleep at bay.

Since she moved to town, life had been full of enjoyment and peace. Then Josh arrived. Now everything seemed hollow.

She should never have allowed herself to fall in love with him, and she vowed she would dismiss him from her thoughts. But try as she might, she was unable to erase thoughts of him from her mind. Words circled inside her head. *Security. Trust. Risk. Faith.*

What did she want? A safe place free of fear? Fear had been ever present on the farm. Yet, deep down, she knew that, among her family, only she had felt that gut-wrenching worry about what they'd eat and how they'd live. More than once Mother had assured her, "We don't have a lot but we'll get by. And things will get better."

But she hadn't stopped agonizing until she got her job with Doc and found this house.

Security is not found in a place, position, or possession — but in God.

The words bolted into her mind. Where had she heard them? Luke, of course. What else had he said? Something about faith being revealed by one's choices. But did taking risks prove one's faith?

She was certain it did not. Still, she was forced to admit that refusing to take risks didn't reveal faith either. God had provided this situation for her in answer to her prayers. And it was warm and cozy. Like a cocoon.

She bolted upright in bed.

It was true. She was trusting her situation for security. No longer did she cry out to God to meet her needs. She shivered, feeling suddenly lost.

But God hadn't changed. She had. She took a deep breath and lay back down. She was glad of this reminder of what she truly believed. Security was found in God alone.

God, I don't know what's right anymore. I thought I was right to appreciate what You have provided. But I fear that I am finding it too comfortable and not as enjoyable as I once thought. I love Josh and miss him already. Are You leading me into a new adventure? Is my lack of faith keeping me from considering the life of a pioneer wife? God, please bring him back.

She lay quietly for a moment and let her anxiety ease away. A new resolve grew within her. Wherever God led her, she would contentedly go. Even if it meant leaving town, this house, and the job she had come to love.

Her heartbeat quickened and she pressed her palms to her chest as she admitted that which she had been pushing away: to share a new life with Josh would not require one ounce of sacrifice.

Still, it was too late to think of such a thing. She'd thrown away her chance with Josh. If only she hadn't been so blind. She'd learned her lesson too late. An aching hollowness echoed through her thoughts.

With the dawn of a new day, she crossed the street and headed up the path to Doc's house. A white petal on the ground riveted her attention and she tipped her head to see the Mayday tree in a garment of white, heavy-scented blossoms. But the scent triggered no answering song in her heart. The branches were full of birds exulting in spring, but there was no response in her heart. Spring had lost her song, when only a few days ago creation had rung with music and happiness.

She moaned. Without Josh, life lay before her muted and bland. Turning away, she slowly climbed the steps, her head dipped close to her chest.

Dora entered the sickroom and she crossed to the bedpost where Josh's saddlebags hung. With trembling fingers she caressed the smooth leather, hungrily breathing in the scent.

Perhaps he would return for his belongings.

The next day, when afternoon office hours were almost over, a young boy clamored in from outside and ran to where his mother sat, waiting to see the doctor. "Mom, guess what? A man just rode up to the sheriff's with two men tied up in ropes. They sure looked mad, too."

Dora smiled at his enthusiasm, knowing that the activity of town was new and exciting for the boy.

Shortly, Dora announced to Doc, "That's the last of today's patients." But, before she finished speaking, she heard the clatter of boots on the steps.

Doc groaned. "Not quite, lassie."

The door flung open and Dora gasped. Josh stood facing them, breathing hard.

Dora knew her mouth hung open but she couldn't stop staring. Nor could she find her voice.

Josh's gaze held Dora's until she thought she was drowning in something unfamiliar — yet comforting. Doc broke the spell as he spoke. "We thought you had headed west, my boy."

Josh blinked and turned to face the older man. "Sorry about that, Doc. I hadn't planned to ride away without so much as a good-bye."

Dora couldn't stop looking at Josh. She noted the smudge of dirt along one cheek, the white sun-squint creases that radiated from his eyes, and the way the sun had frosted his eyelashes. And then she was looking into his warm brown gaze again, lost in a thousand sensations that sent her heart rocketing from height to depth. Seeking equilibrium, she tried to tear her gaze away but found she could not. She knew this unsettled state would last until she could explain how she'd changed her mind.

What if Josh has changed his mind as well? The painful thought caused her chest to tighten until she could barely breathe.

"I went out to ride and think, but I soon discovered that I wasn't alone on the road. I caught sight of the two men who had robbed me." Josh continued to watch Dora. "I was near certain that they weren't following me, but I decided to round up the varmints and bring them to justice." He shrugged. "It took longer than I expected to circle round and get the drop on them." At his crooked grin, a tremble raced across Dora's shoulders.

Doc harumphed. "I best go see how Mrs. Mac is doing. She'll be glad to know you're back." He turned on his heel and left the room.

Dora took a deep breath. God had blessed her with another opportunity and she wasn't going to waste it. But before she could speak, Josh stepped closer.

"I had plenty of time to think while I was gone," he began. Josh's eyes darkened as he studied her face with a hunger that made her cheeks warm. She swallowed hard, hopelessly trying to corral her thoughts. The power of his nearness turned her emotions into a tumult. She held her breath for a moment trying to slow the quivering of her insides long enough to say the words she'd practiced half the night.

Josh looked down at his hands. The sudden loss of his gaze gave her a rash of goose bumps. Then he looked once more into her eyes, his expression so serious she could feel her pulse under her tongue.

"I don't want to go anywhere without you. Doesn't matter how pretty the country is — without you it is nothing." He paused and the silence thundered in her ears. "I've decided to get a job in town and live here." His Adam's apple bobbed. "That is if you meant it when you said you loved me."

He would give up his dream for her! He was willing to live in town!

She caressed the idea for a moment and found that it gave her no pleasure. God had surely done a work in her heart. A glow began somewhere behind her heart and radiated to her toes, her fingers, her face. It made her want to laugh and cry and shout all at the same time.

"I meant it when I said I love you, Josh." Her voice shook. "But I don't care where we live or what you do." She grinned as his eyes grew round.

"I don't understand."

Her smile widened. "I've had plenty of time to think as well. And I prayed that God would give me another chance to tell you — I will go with you to the farthest mountains if you still want me...."

He didn't wait for her to finish but wrapped her in a hug and swung her off the floor, yelling, "Yahoo." She was gasping when he set her on her feet, his arms still circling her. He dipped his head in order to look into her face. "Are you sure about this?"

"As sure as can be. I realized life in town was a life of quiet desperation if it meant giving up the love of a lifetime." She had learned so much more and someday she'd tell him. Someday, but not now.

He nodded, still serious. "Even so, I'm willing to live in town. I don't want you to be unhappy."

She shook her head. "That is not necessary." She realized she had turned a corner in her thinking and was no longer afraid to face change or even uncertainty. Excitement replaced her fear.

"I don't want to miss the adventure of a lifetime."

His arms tightened, pressing her to his chest. She rested her face against his dusty shirt, listening to the steady beat of his heart. With warm fingers he tipped her head back.

"Dora Grant, I love you with all my heart. Will you marry me and make my life complete?"

She smiled up at him, listening to the song in her heart. "Josh Rivers, I love you more than anything, and I will marry you and follow you to the ends of the earth. Your love is my song."

He laughed low in his throat. "We'll only go as far as the foothills." Sobering quickly, he added, "I will sing you a love song every day."

She sighed and placed her ear against his chest again so that she could hear his heart.

"This is my love song . . . ," she whispered. As was his smile, his voice, his touch. Each new day with Josh would bring a fresh love song.

He caught her chin in his palm and turned her face upward. "I love you so much, Dora." His lips, warm and possessive, found hers. She tangled her fingers in the curls at the back of his neck, letting her kiss say what her heart felt.

He lifted his head. "Ah, my sweet, sweet Dora. I can't imagine life without you." Their gazes sought and held each other for many long moments before he stepped away, catching her hand. "I've something to show you." He drew her to the sickroom and snagged his saddlebags from the end of the bed. Flipping them onto the quilt, he dug into his trousers' pocket for a knife. He flicked open the blade and jabbed it into the side of a saddlebag, ripping open the seam.

Dora gasped as a false back opened up and paper money spilled forth.

Josh stood back and grinned, his hands on his hips. "This is what those men were after. There's more in the other bag. More than enough to build a house and start a herd of the best English cows." He sobered, studying her closely. "I thought about what you said — how some people risk everything and sometimes lose it. And you're right. So I propose to put half of this in a bank account as our nest egg. That way, should disaster strike, we'll have enough to start over."

She wanted to say that such a plan wasn't necessary; they could depend on God, but she knew he was right. Her heart was ready to burst. Barely able to speak, she whispered, "You are a very wise man. No wonder I love you."

His lips warm and gentle, he kissed her again. Then he pulled away and grabbed her hand. "Let's go tell Doc and Mrs. Mac."

She laughed, a breathless sound of pure joy. Somehow she didn't think the good doctor and his wife would be surprised to hear how things had turned out.

About the Author

LINDA FORD

Linda draws on her own experiences living in the Canadian prairie and Rockies to paint wonderful adventures of romance and faith. She lives in Alberta, Canada, with her family, writing as much as her full-time job of taking care of a paraplegic and four kids who are still at home will allow. Linda says, "I thank God that he has given me a full, productive life and that I'm not bored. I thank Him for placing a little bit of the creative energy revealed in His creation into me, and I pray I might use my writing for His honor and glory." She has had three novels published with Heartsong Presents.

The Barefoot Bride

Linda Goodnight

Introduction

The Barefoot Bride by Linda Goodnight
The widow Emma Russell is crazy, according to the people of Goodhope. But the talk doesn't scare off Matt Tolivar, who answers the widow's intriguing ad for a husband. Perhaps on a secluded Kansas homestead he can finally escape the past that torments him.

Chapter 1

Goodhope, Kansas, 1883

Husband wanted. Must be God-fearing, hardworking and clean.

Dr. Matthew Tolivar frowned as he read the carefully lettered sign hanging inside the door of O'Dell's General Store. Removing his battered hat, he swiped a hand through his dark hair, a shaggy reminder of the weeks spent on the road. A second swipe, this one over his square jaw, grated against several days' growth of whiskers.

"What kind of woman would advertise for a husband?" he muttered, half to himself.

"A crazy one."

Matthew turned slowly toward the speaker. The little man stood behind a long, rough-hewn counter, surrounded by an odd assortment of horse tack, yard goods, and canned foods. *Crazy.* His crude answer echoed in Matt's head. *Yes,* he thought, *or desperate.* And Matt Tolivar knew about desperate.

"Name's O'Dell. Jimmy O'Dell. I'm the proprietor here." The storekeeper's woolly tufts of red hair circled his balding head like a fuzzy horseshoe. "You'd be new in town, I'm guessing. Most folks from these parts know all about Emma Russell and her crazy ways."

"So this quest for a husband is just part of her dementia?" Matt let his hat dangle in one hand as he surveyed the store. It reminded him of a hundred other stores he'd visited in his wanderings.

He stifled a weary sigh. He was tired of running. Tired of always being a stranger. Tired of being alone. A situation like his made even a crazy woman's offer sound good.

"No. No," O'Dell answered, "Emma's after a man, all right. That big old farm won't run itself, and she's just a little bit of a woman. Can't do it alone. But her sign's hung there for a year or more, and only the new folks pay it any mind. I just leave it up for conversation. Once in awhile some fella takes a notion to head out that direction. Six sections of prime grazing land is a mighty big temptation, you know?"

"Why doesn't she just hire someone?"

"She's touched, I tell you. Young Dan Barton worked for her a bit, and she nearly scared the poor boy to death. 'Possessed,' he said. She was dancing with brooms and talking to the air." He shook his head, foreboding in his expression. "I saw Dan myself, come running into town one day, white as St. Patty's ghost. Since then, the townsfolk keep their distance. No telling what that woman might do."

"Dancing and talking never hurt anyone. Is she dangerous?" Matt was curious. In his days as a physician, the insane had stirred his heart to compassion. Though the common practice was to put them away, Matt had remembered the compassion of Jesus toward the sick in soul and mind. How could a physician do less than try to help them? Sometimes treatments worked; sometimes they didn't. But Matt had always tried.

"You wouldn't be thinking of going out there, would you?"

Was he? Matt didn't know for certain. While he considered the question, a curtain behind the counter parted and a copper-haired woman stepped out, sea green eyes flashing. "Da, are you talking about Emma again?"

"Now, Maureen . . ." O'Dell grinned at Matt. "This avenging angel is my daughter, Maureen. Always she's fighting for those she pities."

Maureen laughed. "An angel, he's calling me. And the two of us always quarreling over something." She came around the counter, pink skirts swaying. "And who might you be, Mr. . . . ?"

"Tolivar," he said. "Matthew Tolivar."

Maureen snitched a peppermint stick from a jar on the counter and aimed it at him. "Well, Mr. Tolivar, don't you go listening to this da of mine. Emma Russell is a gentle woman who's had more suffering than the Lord should allow, and this town has turned its back on her instead of helping out."

"Maureen." Her father scowled at her from behind the cash register. "Don't be getting none of your funny notions. That woman never belonged here in the first place. Old Jeremiah Russell had no business sending off for a mail-order bride. We all told him no good would come of it. Only the demented or desperate would consider such an offer." O'Dell shifted his gaze to Matt. "She was an orphan, you see. And old Jeremiah needed someone to help him care for that big old place of his. Orphans got bad blood, we told him. And we was right." He pursed his lips and gave a knowing jerk of his head. "Now that Jeremiah's dead, we folks in Goodhope have to keep our eyes and ears open lest that crazy widow steal our children or murder us in our sleep."

"Emma would never hurt a soul, Da." Maureen tossed her head, and a red curl bounced down upon one shoulder.

"You're the only one who believes that, girlie. Now, you mind what I've told you and stay clear of her, or I'll be tearing a strip off ya."

The harsh warning brought a flush to Maureen's pretty face. Rebellion burned in her eyes, but she gnawed silently on the candy stick.

A tiny seed of compassion sprouted in Matt's chest, both for Maureen and the Widow Russell. No one knew better than he did about being an outcast, about suffering the sly, speculative glances of his neighbors.

"Where does this widow live?" Matt asked, more curious than ever about the woman. "I could use a day or two of work."

"Just like the sign says." Maureen spoke quickly, casting a defiant glance at her glaring father. "Take the road north out of town about three miles and follow the creek to a stand of cottonwoods. 'Tis the only house for miles."

"Maureen, this young feller can find work somewheres besides there. Now, hush your jabbering and go help your ma with the little 'uns. She's feeling poorly this morning."

From the attached rooms in the back came the noise of playing children. Maureen slanted a glance in that direction, then gave a saucy shrug and disappeared around the curtain.

Shaking his head, O'Dell said, "That girl has a heart of gold but doesn't know what's good for her. I 'spect she sneaks off to that crazy woman's house, though I can't catch her at it. Thank the good Lord she's devoted to her mama, or there's no telling what kind of nonsense she'd get into."

"I'm sorry your wife's feeling poorly. I hope her ailment isn't serious." He clamped his teeth together to keep from asking if the woman needed his services. Thankfully, the storekeeper didn't notice.

"Nah, same as always when she's expecting. Sick in the mornings, sleepy all day. After ten of the darlin's, though, she's an old hand at it. Be right as rain in a few months."

A sick ache, worse than the grippe, pulled at Matthew's belly. Visions of Martha rose to haunt him, her body round with his child. Martha, his own wife, the one patient his skilled medical hands couldn't save. He gulped back the wave of guilt and sorrow that was never far away.

"I hope Mrs. O'Dell feels better soon,

sir," he said, shifting to safer ground. "Now, if you don't mind, I'd like a tin of sardines and a few crackers to take along for my dinner."

The Irishman scuttled around, his boots scraping on the wooden floor, as he gathered up the items and pushed them across the counter.

"Plan on staying in town long, Mr. Tolivar? 'Tis a nice little settlement. Folks are friendly. Plenty of opportunity for a hard worker." He took the coin Matt handed him, testing it between his teeth. Satisfied, he poked at the cash register until the drawer chinged open. "I suppose that Russell woman is the only blight on the whole county, and she knows better than to show her face in town too often. Stay clear of her, and you'll get along fine around here."

Matt didn't appreciate the not-so-subtle warning. He was a man who took care of himself and made his own decisions. Whoever this Russell woman was, she led a hard, solitary life — an existence as lonely and empty as his. That fact alone won her his sympathy.

Matt looked over his shoulder at the faded paper. Suddenly, it took on new meaning. The Widow Russell needed a husband and a ranch hand. Matt Tolivar needed a place to hide and a purpose in life. Maybe they could work out a deal.

With his lunch in one hand, he clapped on his hat and headed for his horse.

The people of Goodhope were right. Emma Russell was crazy.

Barefoot, she danced in circles around the early stalks of green corn standing tall in her garden. Her laughter bubbled up and echoed over the vast grasslands surrounding her ranch.

"Thank you!" she called, voice loud and joyous, though Matt knew for certain she wasn't talking to him. "How can I ever thank you enough?"

Whirling wildly, her plain calico skirts flapped against the cornstalks and made a *whap, whap, whapping* noise. "I do declare that's the prettiest sound in all the world. Don't you think so?"

She was turned sideways, talking to the corn or some unseen visitor.

Matt tied his horse to the rough-barked rail running along the front porch of her cabin and waited for her to notice him.

Watching her now, he wondered why he'd bothered to come out here. He'd been warned. But after six years of roaming the frontier, he was too weary to travel on. Besides, he'd long since discovered that a man couldn't outrun his own conscience.

"Ah, would you look at that?" she said to the warm May breeze. "He's back, the little rascal."

For a moment, Matt thought she spoke of him. Then he saw the rabbit hopping toward the garden. To his surprise, instead of flapping her skirts to chase the varmint out of her corn, she pulled a young green stalk and laid it on the ground in the animal's path.

"Now, maybe you'll leave the rest alone."

With a smile as pretty as Maureen O'Dell's, the crazy widow hefted the hoe and started toward the cabin, singing and chattering all the way. Halfway there she looked up, spotted him waiting in the cool shade, and stopped to appraise him.

"Lovely day, isn't it?" she asked simply, as though the sight of him standing in her shade was a common one.

"Yes, ma'am," Matt answered in the same matter-of-fact manner, then he stepped forward, removing his hat. He had expected her to be old and ugly as a witch, but she was neither.

"Did you see Noah, then? He's gathering in the animals, two by two."

Her words brought Matt to a halt. He blinked in confusion. Didn't seem to be anyone around but him and her. She *was* crazy. He had to be careful until he knew the extent of her dementia.

"Oh, you have to see him," she insisted. "Come on. I'll show you."

As she crossed the yard, a beatific smile greeted Matthew from beneath honey-colored eyes that matched her hair. Back home in Virginia, women had creamy pale skin, carefully protected from the sun, and their hair was neatly groomed on top of their heads. Emma Russell's skin was as golden brown as freshly baked bread, and she wore no bonnet on the wild, windblown hair that flowed freely over her shoulders and down her back. Her arms and neck were as bare as her feet. She was oddly beautiful in a wild, earthy manner that reminded him of the untamed mustangs he'd seen in his journey across the plains.

As she reached his side, bringing with her the fresh green scent of growing things, she took his hand as easily as if they'd grown up together. Too surprised to pull away, Matt let her lift his arm and point it toward a huge, fluffy configuration of white fair-weather clouds.

"Right there. See?" she said. "It's Noah,

I'm certain. See his staff? And that long, flowing beard?"

A chuckle worked its way up inside Matt's chest, but he repressed it. Like a child, the Widow Russell was forming pictures in the clouds. Her insanity was most likely harmless, a return to childlike ways.

"Maybe it's Moses, striking the rock," Matt said, responding to her game. How many years had passed since he'd done such a silly, lighthearted thing?

"You could be right." She dropped his arm and turned to face him with those pale gold eyes. "Are you a God-fearing man, then?"

"Yes, ma'am." The remnants of his faith were all that kept him going, though he'd long since stopped bothering God with his day-to-day worries.

"Good. Good. He wouldn't send any other kind, now would He?"

Matt blinked at her, baffled. "Who?"

"Why, the Lord, of course."

"Oh. I suppose not." *What is she talking about?*

"He told me you were coming. I just didn't know when." She leaned the hoe against the side of the porch. "Come on in."

"Who told you I was coming?" He followed her across the porch ducking his head to miss the dangling onions hung in bunches from the rafters. "The Lord?"

Emma turned back, her gaze moving over him as softly as the breeze, which lifted the tendrils of hair from her forehead.

"I've waited two years for you to get here, and now that you've arrived, I can tell you're the right one. God wouldn't send anyone but the best."

She talked crazy, and her behavior was unusual, but her calm, amber eyes looked as sane as any he'd ever held in his gaze.

"Come in. I'll fix us a nice lemonade while we talk."

Matt asked himself again why he didn't just get back on his horse and ride away. But for some strange reason — most likely his medical curiosity — this woman fascinated him.

Or could it actually be the Lord's doing, him being here? Could Emma be right? Did God work that way?

Somewhere from the past he remembered the saying, "God works in mysterious ways, His wonders to perform."

Well, Emma Russell and this bizarre situation were certainly wonders.

He followed her inside, noting how large the cabin was compared to most he'd seen. She led him through a small parlor. A rocking chair and a cradle sat beside the fireplace and colorful rag rugs covered the plank floor. The place was homey. Pleasant and cozy. The kind of home where a man could put up his feet and relax after a hard day's work. The kind of home that Matt hadn't had in a very long time. As he considered the cleanliness, he thought it unlikely that an insane mind could bring such order. Could the people of Goodhope be wrong about the Widow Russell?

Graceful as a deer, Emma moved about the kitchen, her hair catching the sunlight now streaking in between the yellow curtains. Matt settled at the round oak table to watch and found the experience much more pleasant than he could have imagined. She emanated a gentleness, a peace that stirred him in ways he'd long since forgotten. What was it about her?

"I'm Matthew Tolivar," he said, breaking the silence and his own wayward thoughts. "I saw your sign at the store in town."

"And?" She handed him a cool glass, then took one for herself before sitting across from him, as calm and rational as he.

"Why do you want a husband?"

She sighed, a breathy sound that raised the hair on Matt's arm and made him even more aware of Emma Russell's peculiar loveliness. When she began to speak in a low, sweet voice, he set his glass aside and leaned forward, suddenly eager to be convinced, not only of her sanity, but of her need for a husband.

"Two years ago, a blizzard hit this part of Kansas and lasted for weeks."

"The blizzard of '81." Everyone knew about that terrible time when men froze in their saddles and cattle froze in the fields.

"We thought we were safe and snug here in the cabin — my husband Jeremiah, Lily, our little girl, and me. Jeremiah wasn't a young man, but day after day, he stumbled from the house to the barn, taking care of the stock, bringing in wood. He was so good, so kind. He'd never let me go out there." Absently, Emma drew circles on the table with her glass. "I wasn't surprised when the fever struck him, just scared. Then, soon after, Lily took sick. The wind kept blowing and the snow piled higher. I couldn't go for help." She glanced up. "Goodhope has no doctor, even if I could have gotten out. There was nothing I could do but pray and wait."

A lump formed in Matt's throat. He didn't want to hear this; didn't want to be reminded of his own lost family. He sipped at the tart drink, washing down bitter memories. He'd asked. Now he had to listen.

"Lily was so small, she couldn't fight the sickness. Her little chest closed up so tight that all the mustard plasters in the world couldn't open it up again."

"Pneumonia?" Matt asked quietly, recognizing the strangling symptoms.

Emma nodded, her voice small and distant. "One night, I sat beside her bed, listening to the howling wind and counting every breath my baby took. Soon, there was only the wind, blowing, blowing, blowing."

The tortured story pulled at Matt. He knew just how hard the loss of a child could hit a parent.

"I'm sorry, Mrs. Russell." As he'd done many times with his patients, Matt reached out and lay his hand over hers. She didn't pull away and a warmth crept from her small, weathered hand upward to his icy heart.

"I know," she ventured a sad smile. "So am I. Jeremiah died the next day, and there I was, all alone in a cabin with my dead family while the blizzard raged on."

"How long before help came?"

"I don't rightly know, Mr. Tolivar." She shook her head and looked away. "You see, for a while, I lost myself. I know how that sounds. That's why the townsfolk still think I'm crazy to this day. It's hard to explain, and I don't expect you to understand. But my whole world caved in when Jeremiah and Lily died."

Yet, Matt did understand. He knew how grief could tear away at the inner man until he was so lost he couldn't find his way back. Hadn't the same thing happened to him in a different way? Hadn't he roamed the plains, searching for something, and all the while that something was within him?

"Grief does strange things," he said kindly.

"In those dark, terrible days after Jeremiah and Lily died, I prayed to die with them. Why should I, with nothing and no reason to live, remain here, when they, who were so good and perfect, were gone? But finally, as I lay on my empty bed one night, the sweetest presence filled that room." She smiled softly, an inner radiance lighting her eyes. "It was Jesus."

Jesus? Matt stiffened, struggling to keep his expression bland. "What did He say?"

"Say?" Emma seemed to come back from a distant place. She tilted her head to the side and shrugged one thin shoulder. "Oh, He didn't say anything. He just stood there, watching me with His wonderful, kind eyes and letting His peace flow around me like a great cleansing river of light. When I woke up the next morning He was gone, but He'd left behind such a strength and joy that I could no longer lie in bed feeling sorry for myself. God had given me life and Jeremiah had given me this place. I had to do right by both of them."

A dream. That was all. In her grief, she confused a dream with reality. Matt breathed a quiet sigh of relief.

Emma slipped her hand from beneath his and inhaled deeply. "That, Mr. Tolivar, is why I need a husband. Jeremiah left me a fine ranch, but I cannot run it alone. Hired men are either dishonest or afraid of me. They think I'm crazy, you see. Maureen says that some folks in town believe I should be put away and my land sold. A husband can keep that from happening."

Matt set his glass on the table and scooted his chair back, meeting her gaze. "According to the law, Mrs. Russell, a woman's property belongs to her husband. Had you considered that?"

She twisted her hands nervously in her lap. "Yes. I know. That's why I have to find the right person. An honest man who'll do right by me. I've prayed a very long time. And now you've come."

Matt wanted to promise her, then and there, that he'd always take care of her. He didn't know why. The idea didn't make a lick of sense to him. Perhaps her sad story struck a tender chord in his own sick soul. Whatever the reason, he knew he would stay. And he knew he would marry the crazy Widow Russell.

Chapter 2

Matthew awoke to the sound of voices. No, not voices. One voice. A sweet, feminine voice somewhere below.

"Daisy dear," the voice said. "What would I do without you?"

From his prickly bed in the hayloft Matt opened one eye and peeked through the missing planks in the barn roof at the first pink-gray hint of morning. Slowly, memory returned to his sleep-fogged mind as he recalled where he was and what he'd agreed to do. Last night, over the best home-cooked meal he'd had in months, he'd consented to marry a woman who, this very moment, was somewhere below him, babbling to herself like a lunatic.

"The Anderson children will appreciate this so much. There are four of them, you know, and children are always hungry." She laughed softly. "But you're taking care of that, aren't you, dear heart?"

Quietly, Matt edged toward the sound until he was lying on his belly peering down at the top of Emma Russell's head. Now he saw what he couldn't see from his bed of hay. She was talking to a sleek, docile Guernsey cow while her small hands rhythmically squirted milk into a gleaming bucket.

"Thank you, Lord, for Daisy." The conversation suddenly switched to prayer, an unsettling habit Matthew had encountered more than once the previous day. "And thank You for sending Matthew Tolivar my way. He's the right one, I know. Though I never expected him to be quite so handsome."

Matthew held his breath, listening. Handsome, was he?

"But I don't mind a bit, Lord, that looking at him is pleasant. Especially since he's sturdy built with shoulders strong enough to do the things around here that I'm too small to do."

A curl of pleasure rose in Matt's belly, warming him like smoke rising from a chimney on a chilly day. She thought he was strong and handsome. For the life of him, he didn't know why her opinion mattered. But it did.

"And his blue eyes, Jesus, as pretty as a summer day, but so full of sadness. You know his secrets. You know what's hurt him. Help him find the peace he needs."

A familiar heaviness descended upon Matthew, erasing all pleasure in Emma's rambling over his good looks. He had come here to hide, to bury himself in hard, mind-numbing work; hoping to blot out all memory of who he was and what he'd once considered his calling in life. By helping the poor widow, he could make amends for his own failure and never have to think of medicine again. That alone was reason enough to marry her. It didn't matter if she thought him as plain as a stick.

Wearily, he rose and thumped back to his bedroll, making enough noise to warn Emma that he was awake. The black medical bag he'd used as a pillow more times than he could remember now mocked him as he rolled it tightly inside the woolen blankets. He stopped, unrolled the bedding, and stashed the bag in the far corner of the loft beneath a pile of hay. He wouldn't need the bag or its contents ever again. He didn't know why he'd kept it so long, except that his selling it might raise questions he didn't want to answer. Someday, a traveling peddler would come along, and he'd be rid of the bag for good. For now, he didn't need the reminder of all he'd lost. Today, he'd start a new life and leave the old one behind forever.

There was plenty here to keep his body busy and his mind preoccupied. The Widow Russell had done her best to keep things going. He could see that. Even the barn was neatly kept, the hay raked to one side, fresh straw in the stalls. The animals were healthy and well fed, the garden planted and sprouting. But everywhere he'd noticed signs that the job was too big for her to tackle all alone. The barn door sagged to one side. A half-finished row of fence trailed from the barn to nowhere. And the woodpile was woefully low. No doubt, a further inspection would reveal more, and he was glad for that. Glad for the opportunity to hang up his hat and exhaust himself at something worthwhile.

Buttoning his shirt, he descended the ladder. The widow heard him coming and looked over one shoulder.

"Are you ready for some flapjacks?" Emma asked as she spread a clean white cloth over the brimming milk bucket.

"Sounds good." Matt took the pail from her hands. "I'll wash up a bit first, if you don't mind. You did specify clean in your advertisement, didn't you?"

"Did you hear that, Jesus?" With a merry laugh, Emma reclaimed the milk bucket and led them out of the barn, her yellow dress a bright spot in the early morning.

Matt followed behind, shaking his head. Just when he'd decided that only a logical, rational woman could have kept the farm going so long, she talked to a cow or a rabbit or the Lord Himself, raising fresh questions and doubts in his mind.

"How long have you been up?" He stopped to scrub himself at the well where Emma had placed a rag and sliver of soap in anticipation of his needs.

"Awhile. I love the hours before sunrise when the stars are still out and the rest of world is sleeping. You can see things in the darkness that are never around in the daylight." She set the milk on the wooden ledge of the well and drew the water bucket to the top. Pouring a bit of the liquid on a rag, she rinsed her hands and swiped her grass-covered feet. The hem of her gingham dress was dew-drenched, letting him know that she'd been farther than the barn this morning. He couldn't help but wonder where she had gone in the darkness. Did she roam the woods baying at the moon or communing with the devil?

Matt shoved the damp hair back from his forehead and dismissed the ridiculous notions. The conversation with the storekeeper had filled his head with nonsense. He was a man of science, not an ignorant country bumpkin who believed the insane were all devil-possessed. Emma Russell was a Christian woman. Of that he was certain. And with each minute spent in her company, he became more convinced that the town of Goodhope was wrong about her mental state.

Tossing the towel over one shoulder, he hefted the two buckets and followed her to the house. A half-dozen red chickens clucked around the front porch, running full speed toward Emma when they saw her coming.

"Not yet, girls. But give me six eggs today, and there will be corn for everyone this evening." To Matt she said, "Just set the milk on the sideboard, please, and sit down. I'll have breakfast ready in no time."

Ignoring her command, Matt strained the milk, set it to cool, and rinsed the bucket, hanging it upside down on a nail by the back door. If he was going to live here, he might as well let her know he wasn't lazy.

Emma opened the cookstove and poked at the fire, then she rubbed an iron skillet with lard before clapping it onto the stovetop. Pancake batter sizzled against the hot skillet and the smell of sausage set Matt's belly to rumbling. He'd missed this. Missed the familiar warmth and smell of a kitchen and a pretty woman bustling around, preparing a meal.

"Mrs. Russell."

"Might as well call me Emma."

"All right, Emma." He sipped at the coffee she handed him and wondered when he'd last drunk from anything but a tin cup. "I reckon I'll go into town later and fetch the preacher."

Her hands stilled. "You're still agreeable, then?"

"If you'll have me."

"I will." Drawing in a deep breath, she turned toward him, twisting her hands in her apron. "I got no false notions about this, Matthew. You're marrying me for my land. I'm marrying you to hang on to Jeremiah's dreams and the only home I've ever had. A business agreement, pure and simple. That's all I'm asking. I'll look after you and you look after me."

He heard the relief in her voice when she'd gotten the words out, and he understood her meaning. In Virginia, men and women courted, fell in love, and married, though a few still agreed to arranged marriages. Things were different out here. Men ordered wives through the mail or bartered for them when a farmer had more girls than he could feed. Emma was trying to make it clear to him that she wasn't looking for a love match, just a husband to work her farm. That was fine with him. Absolutely fine. There was nothing left inside him to love.

"People marry for worse reasons," he said, half to convince himself. "We'll do all right, if we set our minds to it."

"Thank you." She piled the flapjacks onto a plate and circled them with sausages. "You're a good man."

"How could you possibly know that?"

"I know." She set the steaming breakfast in front of him. "And Jesus knows."

Matt sighed. There she went again. "And I suppose He told you?"

Innocent amber eyes widened. "How else would I find out?"

How else indeed? But was such a thing possible? Was God the reason that marrying the Widow Russell and resurrecting this farm appealed to him more with each passing moment? Or was it because he could hide here on a farm that other people avoided?

Emma refilled his coffee and placed a jar of molasses next to his elbow. Then she settled into her own chair and plunged into her meal as though she married a stranger every day of the week.

Matthew lifted his fork and looked down at the butter pats on his flapjacks. They were shaped like daisies.

A chink of ice melted in one corner of Matthew's frozen heart. Emma Russell was fanciful, childlike, utterly fascinating, and certainly in need of a man's protection, but he didn't think she was crazy. The more he knew about her, the more she beguiled him, and the more he wanted to stay.

Later that morning, Matt rode away from Goodhope Church, madder than he'd been in years. All the way back to Emma's place he rehashed the conversation with Reverend Jeffers, trying to come up with a winning argument.

"It's against the laws of God and common sense for the insane to marry, Mr. Tolivar," the parson had said as they stood in the sunlight just outside the church where Matt had found him pounding nails in a rickety step.

"I tell you, Reverend, Mrs. Russell is not insane." Matt leaned against the railing and gazed in frustration at the kneeling man. "Unusual and childlike, yes, but as rational and sound as either you or me."

Laying his hammer aside, Reverend Jeffers stood and dusted his hands down the side of his trousers. An angular man with hollow cheeks and burning eyes, he pierced Matt with a look. "Mr. Tolivar, how long have you known Mrs. Russell?"

"Long enough," Matt hedged, hesitant to admit he'd agreed to marry a woman less than a day after meeting her. "And, in my opinion, Mrs. Russell is perfectly sane."

"I see. And by what authority do you judge her mental state?"

"I . . ." Matt stopped and ground his teeth in frustration. As a doctor, he carried the knowledge and authority to make that judgment, but his profession was part of the past, buried when Martha died. He had no intention of resurrecting it. "I've observed her closely," he finished, lamely.

The reverend narrowed his eyes. "Begging your pardon, Mr. Tolivar, but you're a stranger in this town. As the only clergyman for miles around, it's my duty to protect poor Emma from unscrupulous souls who might take advantage of her to gain her land." He held up a bony hand as Matt's expression darkened. "Not that I'm saying you're that kind of man. I don't know you, but I do know Emma. And she has no business making a decision as important as marriage."

"And I'm begging your pardon, Reverend, but this is between Emma and me. All we're asking of you is to perform the ceremony."

"I'm sorry, sir. I cannot, in good conscience, do that. Now, if you'll excuse me," the preacher turned away, "I need to finish this step and get over to the Anderson place."

The dismissal was clear. And so was the message. The Reverend Jeffers would not marry them. Matt crammed his hat onto his head and mounted his horse. The only other preacher was a train ride away, and Matt had no money. He could ask Emma, but most likely all she had was property. Cash was hard to come by.

He stewed over his dilemma the entire three miles back to Emma's place. He thought about praying. Certainly Emma would have. She prayed about everything, talking to God aloud without a bit of embarrassment, then listening with head tilted and expression rapt until Matt was almost sure he could see the Lord whispering in her ear. But that was Emma's way. He was a man, and any man worth his breakfast could find a way without bothering God.

As he rode into the yard, Emma came rushing out the door, amber eyes alight with expectation. When he dismounted and faced her, some of the light faded.

"Parson Jeffers wouldn't come," she said, matter-of-factly.

"No." Resisting the urge to ride back into town and drag the minister to the farm, he tethered his horse to the porch. How did he explain that the preacher thought her too unbalanced to marry? "He didn't think it would be right."

"Well." Emma's delicate face registered only momentary disappointment. "We can't blame the parson. He's only following his conscience."

Matt gave her a solemn appraisal. "Are you saying he's right?"

"To his way of thinking, he is." She pushed a tangle of hair behind one ear and tilted her head, looking up at him. "What about you, Matthew? Do you think I'm crazy? Are you certain you want to be married to a woman like me? Shunned by the town, unable to attend church. Is six sections of land worth that much trouble?"

"Is that what you think? That I'm marrying you just for the land?" Anger, all out of proportion to the question, sizzled inside him.

"Why else then?"

He couldn't honestly answer that question, not if he was to keep his secret, and that bothered him. Even when he'd had little else, he'd kept his honesty. "There are things about me you don't know, Emma. Things that might make you change your mind."

"The Lord sent you. That's all I need to know."

Matt shook his head. Maybe he was the crazy one for considering matrimony with this woman. She talked out loud to Jesus. She accepted a husband she didn't know, and she wouldn't stand up for herself against a town that had badly misjudged her. But then, wasn't that what brought him here in the first place? The crazy widow needed help, and he needed a reason to keep putting one foot in front of the other.

"Then, we'll have to go somewhere else to wed."

With a smile she extended a hand and touched his arm. "Don't fret, Matthew. God will provide a way."

Glancing down at her weathered little hand lying against his sleeve, a new determination overtook him. Instantly, he knew how he would get the money. He'd show the town of Goodhope just how little he cared for their opinion. "There's a preacher up in Dodge who can do the job. Though from what I hear, he does more burying than marrying."

Emma laughed. "Then he needs the practice. And I'd love a train ride to the city."

Just like that she accepted the town's rejection and set her sights in a different direction. Without animosity. Without complaint. If that was crazy, Matt wished the whole world would lose its mind.

As Matt guided the team down Goodhope's narrow Main Street, past playing children, chatting ladies, and the occasional horse and rider, he noticed a strange occurrence. Activity stopped each time one of the townspeople caught sight of him and his companion. Not a single person spoke a word of greeting, but all turned to follow their wagon's progress.

A glance at Emma told him that she noticed too. Head held high, a sweet smile on her lips, she stared straight ahead, but her hands were tightly clenched against her yellow cotton skirt.

Anger surged up in him again. Word must have gotten around that he'd asked the parson to marry them. He yanked the team to a halt in front of the livery and leaped to the ground.

"Emma?" he said, reaching up to her. After a moment's hesitation, she stood and let him swing her down. A woman coming out of the livery gasped, jerked her child against her long skirts and rushed back inside, voice raised.

"Lucas, hurry. That crazy woman is out here."

A young man, tall, lank, with hands the size of shovels appeared at the door. "Now, Mama," he said to the woman. "Why don't you and Patsy go on to the house? I'll see to Mrs. Russell. And thank you kindly for the dumplings. They was mighty tasty."

The woman cast another worried look toward Emma, then hurried away.

"I'm Luke Winchester." The man wiped his hand down the side of his trousers before offering it to Matthew. "And you must be Matthew Tolivar."

Grimly, Matt inclined his head. "News travels fast."

"Yes, sir, it does. Especially when it concerns Emma."

Matt bristled. "She's not deranged."

The stable owner nodded, his expression sympathetic. "I never said she was. But some folks in this town would disagree."

"So I noticed." Matt scowled at the departing woman and child.

"What can I help you with today, Mr. Tolivar?"

With reluctance, Matt reined in his angry

thoughts. No use adding to Emma's embarrassment. "I'll be leaving the team here for a day, maybe a night."

"The bay, too?" Luke asked, indicating Matt's horse tied on behind the wagon.

"He's for sale." Matt jerked a thumb toward the wagon bed. "The saddle, too."

Emma's head shot up, and Matt read the question in her eyes. Why was he selling his horse and saddle?

"A fine piece of horseflesh." Luke walked around the bay, lifting feet, checking teeth. Finally, he named a price.

"You're a fair man, Winchester."

"Yes, sir, I am." He gave Matt the money, counting it into his hand. "I'll take good care of your team, too. You can depend on it."

"Much obliged."

In the distance, a train whistle rent the air. Taking Emma's arm, Matt bid Luke farewell and started toward the depot. With each step down the street, past the barber shop, past the dry goods store, past the apothecary, they were met with the same unfriendly treatment until Matthew felt his blood boil. The storekeeper, O'Dell, had called this a friendly town, but to Matt's way of thinking it was infested with rattlesnakes.

He'd only known Emma two days and

they'd known her for years. Yet, not one of them, unless it was the livery man or Maureen, had an ounce of compassion in them. He wondered how they gathered in that church and prayed with a clear conscience.

As they passed the general store where he'd first seen Emma's sign, the shopkeeper's daughter flew out the door and gripped Emma in a fast embrace.

"Emma, I heard. Is Mr. Tolivar the one, then?" Maureen O'Dell's lilting voice talked about him as though he weren't there. "I'd so hoped he was."

Emma took her friend's hands and together they danced in a circle around the boardwalk, drawing scandalized looks from passersby. Emma didn't seem to notice. "The Lord is good, Maureen."

"Aye, He is." The Irish lass tossed her strawberry hair over her shoulder. Her green eyes settled on Matt as she issued a challenge. "And you'd better be the same, Mr. Matthew Tolivar, or you'll be answering to me, you will."

Again, Matt was amazed that news traveled so quickly, but he understood Maureen's concern for her friend. Life hadn't exactly treated Emma well, and if the town's reception today was any indicator, she sorely needed his protection. "You have my word."

" 'Twill have to do, I suppose." Maureen looked none too convinced. "How will you be wed, with the parson so set against it?"

"We're off to Dodge City on the next train." Still gripping Maureen's hands, Emma gazed up at Matt, gratitude in her face. "Matthew sold his horse and saddle for the tickets."

Matt was not surprised that a woman as sensitive as Emma had quickly grasped his reason for selling, but he wasn't prepared for the unexpected rush of pleasure her appreciation gave him.

"Well, God be praised." Maureen looked at Matt anew. "You'll do, Mr. Tolivar. You'll do fine. Now, be off with you. That cranky conductor suffers no late comers, and I've me ma to tend to."

But Emma wouldn't leave without asking, "How is she, Maureen?"

Worry wreathed Maureen's beautiful face. "She's having a hard time of it. Usually by now the sickness is passed and she's fair glowing with health. But this baby is different, draining all the life out of her, he is."

Matt's gut clenched at the switch in conversation. A sick pregnant woman again. He couldn't, wouldn't let himself think about it too much. He was a farmer now, not a doctor. Such things no longer concerned him.

"I'll be praying for her."

"You do that, Emma, darlin'." Maureen released Emma's hands and stepped back. "Ask Him to send us a doctor while you're at it. The way this town is growing . . ."

To Matt's relief, her words were interrupted by another blast of the train whistle. "Emma," he said, "we'd better go."

Amid a flurry of hugs and warm wishes, Matt found himself embraced by the exuberant Irish woman. "I knew you were bringing good the moment I saw you," she whispered.

Puzzling over the curious words, Matt took Emma's elbow and guided her toward the depot . . . and toward a minister who would make them man and wife.

Chapter 3

The preacher wasn't home.
During their delightful train ride, Emma had entertained Matt and two restless children with her songs and stories and frequent exclamations over the marvels outside the train window. Matt's spirits were considerably higher by the time the train pulled into Dodge. Now, he sat in the parlor of the Reverend Tobias Jefferson drinking coffee he didn't want and listening to Mrs. Jefferson regale Emma with details of her own wedding thirty years ago in Boston.
". . . And my dress, dear child, it was the loveliest thing. All satin and lace with tiny pearl buttons." She paused, enraptured by the memory. "I still have it, you know, tucked away in a chest upstairs. My daughter wanted to wear it when she married, but Clara's tall, and we couldn't lengthen it."
Emma, perched on the edge of the settee, touched the woman's hand in sympathy. "You must have been so disappointed."

"Yes." Mrs. Jefferson sighed. "I always wanted to see it on another bride, but only a little thing like you or me could ever fit in it." Suddenly, she gasped, then popped up from the straight-backed chair, her gaze measuring Emma as she walked a circle around Emma's chair. "Emma dear, stand up."

Clearly bewildered, Emma cast a glance at Matt then stood obediently while Mrs. Jefferson continued her assessment. "Yes . . . yes . . . I do believe it would fit. Your waist is every bit as tiny as mine was. And we're almost the same height."

"Oh, Mrs. Jefferson." Emma's hands flew to her cheeks. "You can't possibly mean . . . you couldn't want someone like me to wear your wedding gown."

"And why ever not?"

Emma's eyes found Matt's. In an hour's time, the crazy widow had thoroughly charmed the preacher's wife, and now she didn't know how to react to the woman's kindness. He could see she wanted this. He could read the eagerness in her face. Not that it mattered one whit to him what she wore. After all, this was no love match and not a soul would care one way or the other if they even got married, but after the ugliness in Goodhope, Matt wasn't about to leave Dodge until Emma was in his legal care. If, while they waited, the young girl within Emma wanted to play dress-up in a thirty-year-old gown it was fine with him.

"I agree, Emma," he said. "Why ever not?"

His approval seemed to be all she needed. With Emma-like enthusiasm, she embraced the older woman. "I would be so honored to wear your dress."

Mrs. Jefferson clapped her hands in delight. "Oh, wonderful! This will be so much fun. Funerals, funerals. That's all we ever have in this town with cowboys shooting each other over everything from whose horse is faster to whose daddy was meaner. You'll be so pretty in that dress. And we'll weave a garland for your hair. And pick some flowers for the church." Excitement seemed to emanate from her every pore. Suddenly, she whirled around and eyed Matt's shaggy hair and whiskered face. "You could use some sprucing up yourself, young man. It's not everyday a woman gets married, and she'd like to see that handsome face of yours, I'm sure."

Surprised by her sudden attack on him, Matt dragged a hand over his prickly jaw. "I suppose I could do with a shave."

"I suppose you could. The barbershop is right down Main Street. You can't miss that red striped pole." With a flap of her hands, she herded him out the door.

As he settled his hat on his head and started down the street, his insides jangling, Matt wondered how the last hour had gotten so out of hand. This wasn't what he'd bargained for, but then, nothing about the crazy widow had been.

When Matthew returned, his face smooth and stinging from the hot shave, he found Emma in the backyard with the parson's wife and a black-suited man he assumed to be the preacher.

"Now, you look more like a bridegroom," Mrs. Jefferson said, approvingly. "And your bride is all ready for you."

The shock of seeing Emma dressed in lace with peach blossoms garnishing her long, flowing hair set his heart to thumping. She waited for him beneath the blooming boughs of a peach tree looking much more like a real bride than he'd expected. Martha had looked like this, radiant, hopeful. He squeezed his eyes shut, bowing his head against the torrent of emotion he did not want to feel and prayed he'd never let Emma down the way he had Martha.

When he opened his eyes again, he noticed what he hadn't seen before, and the sight erased all comparisons to his first wedding. An almost smile threatened his lips. Emma, with her dancing hair and her fancy dress, was barefoot, toes peeking out like a child's, charming him with her sweetness. Peace seeped into him. Taking care of the crazy Widow Russell was the right thing to do. Hat in hand, he went to stand beside his waiting bride.

"Shall we begin?" the pastor asked, opening his Bible.

As the ancient words of faith were spoken, a hush fell over the little gathering, broken only by the hum of insects glorying in the spring. Peach limbs swayed above them, releasing their sweet scent and an occasional shower of blossoms. A pair of robins flitted in and out of the trees tending a nest.

"Will you, Matthew, take this woman . . . ?"

Yes, he would take her as his wife. He would look after Emma and work her land, hiding from his own memories and from the incessant call of medicine on his life. He would promise all that was left of him to Emma Russell, the orphan, the widow, the crazy woman. From this moment on, he'd look forward, not backward.

Gazing down at Emma's upturned face, seeing the hope and trust in her eyes, Matt felt his throat fill and tightened with some unnamed emotion. Swallowing hard, he answered, "I will."

In a whisper that barely reached his ears, Emma repeated her own vows, and while Matt pondered the odd feeling in his chest, the preacher pronounced them husband and wife.

"You may kiss your bride."

Matt and Emma then exchanged equally startled expressions.

At that moment, a yellow butterfly found the flowers in Emma's hair. Matt almost smiled. Emma Russell — he caught himself and nearly smiled again — Emma Tolivar, in satin gown and bare feet, with a butterfly in her hair, had such a strange effect on him. His chest expanded with a sense of satisfaction so profound that he thought he might, indeed, kiss his bride. But before he could, Emma once again surprised them all as she lifted her clear, sweet voice in a hymn of praise.

When the last pure notes of Emma's song faded away, Mrs. Jefferson dabbed at her eyes with a lace-edged handkerchief. "I felt God smiling down on us the entire time. Truly a match made in heaven."

Matt shoved away the disappointment he'd felt when Emma avoided his kiss. After all, Emma had made it clear that theirs was only a marriage of convenience, and he was certainly in agreement with that. But in the last few years, he'd had few special moments to enjoy, and regardless of the circumstances, the vision of his beautiful barefoot bride would stay with him forever. Mrs. Jefferson was right. God must be smiling. And as he glanced down at his radiant new wife, Matthew Tolivar did the same.

Emma felt the effect of Matt's smile all the way to her bare toes. With blue eyes twinkling above the flash of white teeth, her new husband was a devastatingly handsome man. After a stern reminder that theirs was a marriage of necessity, she commanded her fluttery stomach to still. She knew about marriage. If they were truly blessed, they'd get along, maybe enjoy each other's companionship, and some day, they might even share a kindly affection such as she'd shared with Jeremiah. But she had no false notions about love. Still, laughter was good for the soul and Matthew needed to smile more. Out of gratitude for what he'd done, Emma made up her mind, then and there, to see that he did.

Chapter 4

Spring gave way to scorching summer as Matt and Emma fell into a comfortable routine. They worked from predawn to nightfall, sometimes side by side, often apart. There was so much to do, so much which had gone undone. Matt felt the constant pressure of time, determined to get as much fence up as possible before the winter. With fencing, he could raise the thousand or more cattle that Jeremiah had left to roam the open range as well as grow plenty of corn and hay to keep them healthy through the fierce Kansas winters. With hard work, he and Emma could have a secure future, and he'd have no time nor need to think about his forsaken medical practice.

When evening came, he sat in the lamplight, exhausted, hot, and filthy while Emma bustled around getting supper on the table. He enjoyed the evenings, enjoyed watching her do the things a woman did — things a man never even thought of doing. And, not a day passed that she didn't do something that made him smile.

As though privy to his thoughts, Emma handed Matt his meal. A face stared up at him from the blue flowered plate. Two slices of tomatoes formed the eyes. A triangle of ham served as the nose. Thick ovals of bread protruded like ears from each side. And a row of fried okra grinned up at him.

"What's this?" he asked, a half grin tugging his lips.

With a saucy smile, she remarked, "That's the look I'd like to see on your face more often, Mr. Tolivar."

"What!" He returned in mock horror. "Red-eyed? With green teeth? Emma, you have strange tastes in men."

Clearly delighted by the joking reply, Emma threw back her mane of hair, her joyous laugh filling the cabin. Some of Matt's weariness lifted as he dug into his whimsical supper.

When he finished his dinner, Emma's work-worn hands quickly removed the empty plate and set a piece of apple pie and glass of milk in front of him. It was too hot to bake, but Emma had perspired over the stove without a murmur of complaint as though she enjoyed preparing the foods he loved.

"Maureen came out today." Settling into

a chair with a pan of freshly picked peas, she began the tedious job of shelling them. He saw that her fingers were stained green, the nails chipped and ragged. It wasn't the first time he'd noticed the condition of her hands or seen her futilely rub lard into the cracked, dry skin. "She helped me pick these purple hulls."

"Maureen's a good friend," he said, savoring the taste of cinnamon-rich apples. "I trust she's doing well."

"She is. Her mother's having a very hard time, though." Emma paused, resting her forearms on the edge of the pan. "I just wish there was something I could do. . . ." She tilted her head to one side and smiled as though someone had whispered in her ear. "How silly of me, Jesus. As soon as You send us that doctor, we'll know just what to do for Kathryn, and all of us can breathe a little easier."

Guilt shafted through Matt like a knife. Poor Emma, praying for a doctor, and here one sat. His conscience nearly ate a hole through him.

"Maybe she should rest more, keep her feet up."

Emma glanced at him, eyebrows raised in question. Matt shrugged, purposely nonchalant. "I knew a doctor sometime back.

Heard him recommend cutting back on salt and pork and getting plenty of bedrest. She might try that."

"Oh, Matthew, thank you. Maureen will be so relieved, and it certainly wouldn't hurt to try." Emma's ragged little hands resumed their work. "If you're still going into town for supplies tomorrow, I'll send her a letter telling her so."

A measure of relief settled over Matthew as well. He'd helped without revealing his secret, and now maybe he could stop thinking so much about the pregnant woman. *Lord, will the torment never end? Will I never know peace again?*

He swallowed another bite of pie, although the dessert now tasted as bitter as quince. Pushing the plate aside, he leaned his elbows on the table and studied the woman who sat across from him, reviled and scorned, yet filled with serenity. She deserved so much more than public ridicule and a loveless marriage to a man as empty as those pea shells. "Why don't you go into town with me? Visit Maureen awhile. Maybe buy something for yourself."

Her answer was always the same. "No." She shook her head, smiling regretfully. "I wouldn't want to cause trouble."

Though he'd asked her a dozen times,

other than the solitary walks she took through the fields and woods under cover of darkness, Emma refused to leave the farm. Having long stopped thinking she was a lunatic crazed by the moon, Matt suspected where she went on those early morning excursions, though she never told him. If he were right, the town's behavior toward Emma was nothing short of hypocrisy.

"Jimmy O'Dell's an ignorant fool," he said gruffly.

"Matthew," she scolded mildly. "He's a good man, doing the best he knows how to take care of his family."

Matt wanted to argue against the people who refused to give Emma a chance, but he knew better. Every time he broached the subject, she sidestepped him, saying something kind. He'd even heard her praying for them, one by one, as she went about her daily tasks. She was a better Christian than he'd ever be. And far better than the residents of Goodhope.

Matt sighed, knowing that he would travel alone tomorrow.

"It's too hot," he complained, drawing a hand down his gritty neck, "and I'm too dirty to sleep."

With a sudden, merry laugh that startled him, Emma plopped the pan of peas onto the table. She jumped up, dropped her apron over the back of a chair, and flung the door wide open.

"Come on, then," she cried. "I have a wonderful idea."

Having no notion of what he'd said to bring on such a reaction, Matt nevertheless pushed himself back from the table and followed her out into the moonlit night. In their short marriage, he'd come to expect such flights of fancy from his bride. And though others might consider her crazy, Matt found release in the joyful way she embraced each moment. He never knew what to expect, and somehow that added spice to each day.

Once he'd found her lying face down in the backyard and thought she was sick. She shushed him and pulled him down beside her to watch an ant carry a much larger beetle to its hole. Instead of the ant, he'd watched Emma and found the sight of her rapt expression, the glowing golden eyes, and smooth tan skin utterly beguiling. He'd even considered kissing her again, but he'd refrained, remembering their wedding day. That night, he'd lain awake puzzled by the feelings she aroused in him and wondering at the odd sensation hammering in his chest.

"Where are we headed?" he asked. Guided only by the moon and stars, Matt followed her flying hair and billowing skirts to the creek. Beating him there, the ever-barefooted Emma plunged into the cool water.

"Come on. It's wonderful."

Tired as he was, the water would refresh and clean him. And Emma's delightful "craziness" would soothe his weary soul.

As he sat on the rocky bank to remove his boots, Emma waded his direction. By the full moon, he could see she was already soaked, dress plastered to her body, hair streaming. She grinned impishly and flicked water at him. The cold drops felt shockingly good against his parched skin, and he barreled into the creek, splashing and flinging water. Emma laughed and returned fire, soaking him in seconds. Like two otters, they frolicked together, forgetting their aching muscles and tired bodies.

"We should do this every night," he said, shaking back his damp, shaggy hair.

"What? This?" From a running start, Emma gave a shove, pushing him backward onto his backside. Her laughter rang over the tree-lined grove.

"You, dear lady, must be taught some manners." As he groped for a handhold to hoist himself up, Matt made contact with something soft and slimy. Feeling like a schoolboy, he gripped the squirming frog and stalked toward Emma. With a squeal, she floundered toward the bank, but Matt's much longer legs caught her. Holding her captive, he dropped the frog down the back of her dress.

Emma danced around the creek squirming and yelping in mock terror. Her antics brought a chuckle to Matt's lips. In another moment, he was laughing. At the sound, Emma yelped and jumped all the more, fell backwards into the water, splashing and giggling in delight. Dislodged, the hapless frog croaked and bounded toward safer territory.

Sides aching, Matt slogged over to help Emma up. His courtesy was rewarded with a sharp tug that brought him tumbling down beside her. They sat in the water laughing until they were breathless. When at last the silliness passed, Emma looked up at him, her face golden in the moon shadows.

"Listen, Matthew." The croak of frogs pulsated around them. "Even the frogs are laughing."

"Not the one I dropped down your dress. He's sulking somewhere." The silly answer surprised even him.

With a feather light touch on his arm, Emma said, "I like to hear you laugh, Matthew. And so does God."

Matthew Tolivar wasn't given to fanciful notions, nor was he one to dance and cavort in the moonlight. The people of Goodhope would most likely think he'd gone as crazy as his bride, but none of that mattered one little whit. He felt good — good in a way he hadn't felt in a very long time; a fact that puzzled him no small amount.

The strange sensation in his chest returned, and though he was certain there was no room inside him for love, the feeling stayed with him for days.

Bright and early the next morning, Matt hitched up the wagon, loaded it with Emma's milk, eggs, and vegetables, and headed to town. He'd asked her again to go along, but to his disappointment, she had once again refused.

"The scripture says if something we do offends our brother, we shouldn't do it," Emma had said without rancor. "My presence offends them, Matthew."

"That's their fault," he argued. But in the end, she'd stayed behind, waving him off with her ragged little hands.

During the three-mile drive into town,

Matt thought of all the hardship Emma had suffered and determined to try, once more, to make the people of Goodhope see reason. She was the kind of woman who needed people, and though the stubborn townsfolk didn't know it, they needed her zest for life. He was a physician, a trained man of science, who'd lived with Emma for months now. Surely he could convince the people of Goodhope that she posed them no threat. And the best place to start was with her most vocal detractor — the storekeeper, Jimmy O'Dell.

Five minutes into the conversation, Matt knew he was wasting his breath.

"I reckon six sections of land made you an expert on lunatics," Jimmy sneered.

Angered by the insinuation and the man's stubborn refusal to give Emma a chance, Matt was tempted to walk out without the supplies he needed, though it was the only general store for miles. Before he could, Maureen whipped through the curtained door, dragging two redheaded boys by the scruff of their necks.

"Da, it's the woodshed these two are needin' today. Both of 'em running in the house like wild goats, and Patrick here running into Ma and nearly knocking her over."

"I didn't aim to." The accused poked out a defiant lip. "But Danny had a snake!"

Jimmy O'Dell's ruddiness deepened with anger. "You know your ma's not up to such shenanigans from the two of you. Give 'em to me, Maureen. I'll set 'em straight in a hurry if you'll ring up Mr. Tolivar's purchases."

Dragging the recalcitrant boys, the storekeeper banged out the door.

Casting about for a reason to avoid discussing the pregnant woman, Matt spotted a squat white jar on a shelf above Maureen's head. The rose decorated label said MRS. PARKER'S ROSEWATER OINTMENT. "Is that any good?"

Maureen took down the jar, opened it, and sniffed. "Aye, and it smells heavenly, too. See for yourself."

She stuck it under his nose, and the scent of roses enveloped him.

"Emma's hands . . . ," he started, then stopped, embarrassed. "I'll take it."

Maureen cocked her head to one side and stared at him thoughtfully. Then she pulled a bolt of soft green cotton from the shelf, her golden eyebrows arched in question. "She wouldn't mind a new dress now and again either. This color was made for her, I'm thinking."

Emma loved pretty things. Though unlike the women in his past, she owned so few. Her hands needed tending, and there was no telling when she'd made herself a new dress.

He gave a short, self-conscious nod. "All right, then."

"Don't play coy with me, Mr. Tolivar. You're as transparent as glass." With a twinkle in her eyes, Maureen laid the fabric on the counter, tossing in matching thread and lace. "And it's delighted I am to see it."

While Matt grappled to understand her cryptic comment, a faint call came from the back of the store. "Maureen."

"Coming, Ma, in just a minute." Brow puckering, Maureen shook her red curls and spoke to Matt in an undertone. "Six months gone and she's puffy as one of Danny's toads and weak as water gravy."

The worrisome symptoms filtered through Matt's scientific mind. The woman needed a doctor's care, but it wouldn't be him. He couldn't risk the pain of watching another life slip out of his hands. Not now. Not ever.

His thoughts skittered to a stop when Maureen spoke and he realized he'd been frowning toward the curtained doorway.

"Don't you be fretting now, Mr. Tolivar.

The good Lord will provide. With Emma petitioning Him for a doctor, I wouldn't be at all surprised to see one riding into town just any day." Hands and eyes busy with her figuring, she prattled on, unaware of Matt's building anxiety.

Sweat dampened his palms and his heart beat erratically. He needed to get away before he did something irrevocably foolish, like asking to examine the ailing Mrs. O'Dell. Concern for the pregnant woman choking him, Matt managed to gather his purchases, hand over Emma's letter, and make a courteous departure.

"My goodness, you've bought a wagon load," Emma exclaimed, eyeing the bags of flour and meal, the rolls of wire, and buckets of nails. "I'm certain Mr. O'Dell didn't extend credit for all of this."

"It seems Mr. O'Dell is needing meat for his store, so I bartered a bull calf for this and more. He wants me to supply him all through the winter." If there had been any other place to easily sell the beef, Matt would never have bargained with the likes of Jimmy O'Dell. Theirs had been a grudging agreement, brought on by mutual need.

"Praise be to Jesus." Emma ran her hands over the bags, exploring the wagon like an excited child. When she came upon the plain brown package, Matt had a sudden longing to see her reaction. "Open it," he urged.

Eagerly, she released the twine and pulled the paper away. The pale green cloth lay on top.

"Oh, Matt." Her weathered hands caressed the cloth reverently. She lifted the material and held it against her. Maureen was right. The color captured the green flecks in her eyes and turned her hair the shade of ripe wheat.

"Would you look at this, Jesus?" Emma cried, holding the fabric skyward. Suddenly, she began to whirl, spinning, spinning until she became a gold and green blur in the summer sunshine. "Matthew, Matthew, Matthew," she chanted, "you're the kindest man on Earth."

She was a balm for his weary soul, and he laughed to know he could make her happy with such a small gift. Truly it was more blessed to give than to receive, especially when the recipient reacted like Emma.

Breathlessly, she spun to a halt, still clutching the fabric to her chest. Delight shone on her face. Seized by the need to keep it there, Matt said, "There's something else in that package, Mrs. Tolivar."

Back to the wagon she ran, exclaiming over the thread and lace until she came to the jar of Mrs. Parker's Rosewater Ointment. Expression puzzled, she lifted it, turning the bottle in her hands, reading the label, glancing at her mistreated hands.

Seeing her smile disappear, Matt wondered if he'd made a mistake. Was she embarrassed? Insulted? A flicker of anxiety passed over him, but it was short-lived.

Slowly, she uncapped the container, releasing the scent of roses. Eyes closed, she sniffed deeply, head tilted back. When at last she looked at him, tears shimmered above an angelic smile. "Never in my life have I owned anything so wonderful." Swallowing convulsively, she whispered, "Thank you," snatched up the green material, and fled into the house.

That night, long after he'd given up and gone to bed, he heard her humming and murmuring to the rhythm of the sewing treadle. He fell asleep with a smile on his lips and the scent of roses in his nostrils.

He dreamed he heard her, far off, praying. "I love him, Jesus," she said. "Now, what shall I do about that? Him, who should have a fine lady for a wife, one he could be proud of and take to church on Sundays. And here he is stuck with the village outcast, a worthless orphan. A crazy woman. How can I make up to him for all he's done?"

Straining upward against the dark pull of sleep, Matt wanted to say, "You're the one who's good. You're the one who's given me back a reason to live."

But he didn't, of course. It was, after all, only a dream.

The scents of coffee, bacon, and biscuits drifted into Matt's consciousness, and he rose, chagrined that Emma had once again risen long before him. Darkness still covered the farm, though the rooster was singing his anthem. Bare feet thudding on the wooden plank floor, Matt washed and dressed, then stumbled into the kitchen.

"Don't you ever sleep?" he asked blearily, slouching into a chair.

Ever cheerful, she smiled and slid a coffee mug into his hands. "I'm far too excited to sleep."

Then he remembered the cloth and the perfumed ointment. A proud smile twitched at his whiskered face. "Did you sew all night?"

In answer, she left the room, returning momentarily with a green garment that she held up for his inspection. "What do you think?"

To his utter shock, the garment wasn't a dress as he'd expected. It was a carefully crafted man's shirt, as fine as any he'd ever owned.

"But the cloth was for you, for a dress," he protested.

"There's plenty left for that." Brown eyes danced with eagerness. "Do you like it?"

Fingering the soft cloth, Matt swallowed the lump in his throat. Would she never stop surprising him? Would she never stop thinking of everyone else first?

"Ah, Emma, Emma." He pulled her to him in what he thought was a hug of gratitude. In the next instance, he was kissing her. Her soft sweet mouth parted in surprise beneath his, and an emotion far stronger than gratitude hammered in Matt's chest. When he pulled back, stunned and breathless, a pair of luminous golden eyes measured him. She pressed trembling fingers to rose tinted cheeks, then did the unexpected once again.

"How would you like your eggs?" she whispered, then spun toward the stove, turning her back to him.

Matt blinked, baffled at her response, baffled at the desire to kiss her again, and baffled as to why she was talking of eggs when his insides were twisted in a knot. She cared for him. He was certain. Why had she rejected his kiss?

The answer struck him full in the heart. He hadn't been dreaming when he heard Emma say she loved him. The words had been real. Emma loved him, and she knew he had no love inside to give. Guilt gnawed at him. He'd wanted to heal her brokenness, but he'd only caused her more pain.

Chapter 5

Even though the calendar said September, the prairie summer continued in full fury: hot and dry and unforgiving. Sweat bathed both people and livestock as an urgent need for rain pressed in.

The kiss was not mentioned again, though Matt could think of little else. Now that the blinders were off, he saw Emma's love in everything she did, and the burden of responsibility weighed heavily upon him.

Late in the afternoon, a cloud appeared from nowhere, dark and heavy with rain. As the shade passed over, Matt and Emma glanced up, then at each other.

"Wouldn't that be lovely?" Emma called from her back-bent position.

Before Matt could reply, the sky opened and the blessed cool water gushed over the land. Emma squealed and straightened.

"Rain. Wonderful rain."

As Matt watched, rain pouring off his hat, his wife began to twirl and spin, arms wide, face turned upward to the heavens.

"Dance, Matthew," she called, her voice full of joy and laughter. When he only stood with a smile on his face, she ran to him, gathered his hands into her small, rough ones, stood on his boot tops, dipping and swaying. Matt was caught up in her spontaneous delight, her joy too infectious to ignore. To his utter amazement, he wanted to dance and laugh. Emma grabbed his hand and pulled him, captivated, through the mud puddles, stomping and splashing. She could find more happiness in a mud puddle than most people found in their entire lives.

Drenched to the skin, he pulled Emma close to him and looked into her eyes, the urge to kiss her again welling up inside him like an incoming tide. The rain tumbled from his hat onto her face, and she laughed all the more.

"If the people of Goodhope saw us now, they'd say you've gone as crazy as me," she declared, reaching up to swipe a smear of mud from Matt's face.

The cloudburst passed as quickly as it had come and a rainbow split the sky in two.

"Let's chase it, Matthew. And find that pot of gold."

"Ah, Emma. Emma, you're a delight. What makes you the way you are? A woman grown who dances in the rain and lays in the grass at night watching falling stars."

Her laugher ceased and a gentle, wistful sweetness settled over her features. "I thought you knew by now, Matthew."

He could see she was serious, so he waited, holding her close, feeling the combined heat and damp transferring from her body to his, smelling the scent of fresh rain against her skin.

She lay a hand against Matt's cheek and tilted her head to one side, eyes glowing.

"When I was a child in the orphanage, there was no frivolity, no laughter. By the time Jeremiah took me in and taught me of Jesus, all the joy in me was gone. And then I had Lily. She could chase a butterfly for hours, clapping her tiny hands, falling, and getting up with a smile on her face." Emma's voice grew soft with longing. "Oh, Matt, she was my joy. So now, I dance and laugh and sing and do all those foolish things for Lily." Tears of remembrance filled the wide amber eyes. "I dance in the rain for Lily, because she never will."

With his own heart thudding from the poignant beauty of her admission, he finally recognized the truth. He'd come here, thinking he was the healer, the man who could help the poor, crazy widow. But it hadn't been that way at all. It was he who had been healed by Emma's simple faith and her magnificent strength. She had given him back his joy. The truth had been banging at him for weeks, but now he had to tell her.

"I love you, Emma." Feeling her stiffen with shock, he held her all the tighter, kissing away a fat drop of rain clinging to her eyelashes.

"Do you hear me? I love you, Emma," he shouted, laughing anew at the shock on her face that matched the surprise in his heart. "Say you feel the same. I know you do."

And indeed she did. In Emma-like fashion she threw her arms around his neck and kissed him just as the rain began again. Neither of them noticed.

Sunday morning after chores and breakfast, Matthew followed Emma around the cabin, watching her, stealing an occasional kiss, exchanging secret smiles. He was a happy man. Happier than he ever thought possible, and he wanted to be certain Emma was happy too.

"I'm taking you to church this morning," he declared.

Her hands stilled on the towel she was folding. "Oh, Matthew, I don't think so. But if you want to go . . ."

"You once told me how much you enjoyed worshipping with other believers and how much you missed it after Jeremiah died. I think it's time we went together as man and wife."

"But the people . . ." Her throat convulsed, trepidation in her voice.

"I've made a few friends, Emma, and most of the folks are decent. Jimmy O'Dell's the main one who keeps the trouble stirred up. The others just follow along."

"I don't want to upset anyone."

"Once people see you, get to know you again, they'll realize their mistake." Seeing her misgivings, he pleaded, "Please, Emma. If we're going to live and prosper here, we have to find a way to get along with these folks. Both of us — not just me. You're so brave about everything else. Why won't you face this town and make them stop this nonsense?"

"I don't know . . ." She gnawed at her lower lip, clearly weakening.

Matt knelt in front of her, grasping her hand. "What if we have a child together? Wouldn't you want him to be accepted?"

Wonderment lit her face at the possibility, and she capitulated. Drawing in a deep breath, she said, "I'll wear my new green dress."

★ ★ ★

A dozen or so worshipers had already gathered by the time Matt and Emma arrived wearing their matching green. Tipping his hat repeatedly, Matt wove his bride into the church, nodding and smiling, receiving cold looks in return. Beneath his guiding hand, Emma trembled, though she smiled serenely at all she passed.

Matt's pulse thundered. He prayed desperately that he hadn't made a mistake in bringing her here. What else could he do? Somehow he had to give her back her dignity. Searching the gathering for Maureen or Lucas Winchester, he found instead Jimmy O'Dell, bearing down on them, his face livid.

"What is that daughter of the devil doing in the house of God?" He shouted so loud, every head in the building turned to stare. Except for a few murmurs of agreement, the place fell quiet.

"I've told you repeatedly, O'Dell, Emma is mentally sound. She has as much right to attend church as you do."

"Mentally sound, you say?" Jimmy whirled toward the crowd. "You hear that, folks? This stranger comes waltzing into town and tries to tell us our business. Well, I think we got something to say about that, don't you?"

His statement was followed with rumbles of assent. "Yeah. Sure do. You tell 'em, Jimmy."

"Too many people have seen her do crazy things."

"I say she's moonstruck. Barney Adams saw her dancing in a full moon, singing and waving her arms. The next week his good cow died."

Emma stood in the middle, eyes wide, clinging to Matthew's hand. A bearded man in overalls parted the tightening circle.

"She's a witch, if ye ask me." He pointed a finger at Emma. "Seen her myself sneaking around Floyd Anderson's place in the middle of the night just about the time he got hurt. I figure she hexed him."

Matt seethed inside, wanting to tell the real reason for Emma's surreptitious visits to the Anderson place. But when he looked to her for permission, she shook her head in denial. Filled with both frustration and admiration, Matt kept quiet.

The fine churchgoers didn't.

"Mr. Tolivar, you seem to be a good man, hardworking. I've seen the things you're doing to that farm, and I admire you. Your dealings here in town are honest, and we've come to respect you. But when it comes to the widow, you seem blinded, unable to accept that the woman is unbalanced."

"She's evil, all right." This from a squat man with tobacco stained teeth. "I was there when she chased the undertaker and Parson Jeffers off her place, screaming like a banshee."

"She claimed Jesus came to see her."

"What's wrong with you people?" Matt cried. "Emma was sick with grief then. She'd been locked up in that cabin with her dead husband and child without help. Can't you have a little compassion?"

Some of the women softened and made murmurs of understanding. "Losing a child's a hard thing. Any of us would be sick with grief."

"Yes, and you have other children, other family to comfort you. Emma had no one, nothing left at all."

The church was quiet for a moment, and Matt thought that, perhaps, he'd convinced them. Surely the folks could see that Emma was no threat to anyone. But Jimmy O'Dell wasn't finished. "I want her out of here before my wife arrives," he cried, shaking his fist at Matt. "She'll mark my unborn child." He turned to the shocked crowd. "And if she does, the fault will belong to all of you for letting such as her live in this town."

Barely controlling his temper, Matt shoved the fist aside. "You'll mark it yourself with your own ignorance."

Wrapping Emma in his protective embrace, Matt shouldered his way out of the church and into the wagon. Fury, hot and dangerous, emanated from every pore as he slapped the horses into motion, leaving the good citizens of Goodhope in his dust.

"Matthew, please don't be so angry. It's all right. Truly it is." Voice husky with emotion, she lay a hand on his stiff forearm. Her obvious pain infuriated him even more.

"You'll never convince me of that, Emma. Someday they'll reap what they've sown, and I, for one, will be glad." As town disappeared behind them, he slowed the team to a walk. Tall, dry buffalo grass waved in the fields beside the road, and yellow sunflowers nodded their giant heads. For once Emma did not exclaim about their beauty. They rode in silence most of the way home, hurt pulsating from her, remorse filling him. The big red barn came into sight, then the chimney, before Emma spoke again.

"What if they're right?" She stared off into the wheat fields, eyes unseeing. A frown creased her brow. "What if there is something basically bad about me?"

"Don't be foolish."

She turned to him, tears glistening on her lashes, and the sight tormented him. Why had he made her go? He'd vowed to protect her, and instead he'd escorted her into the lions' den to be devoured.

"I know nothing about my mother or father, Matthew," she continued, sadly. "Perhaps I was born in an insane asylum or to a streetwalker."

"None of that has anything to do with who you are."

Tears trickled down her face as her voice rose in sorrow. "Doesn't it? It's all in the blood, they say. Maybe mine is just bad." A sob broke from her throat. "Bad blood. That's what they call it."

"Emma, no." He'd never seen her like this — weeping, heartbroken. He chastised himself anew for subjecting her to such cruel treatment. Pulling the team to an abrupt stop beside the barn, he turned to her. But before he could draw her sobbing body into his arms, she leaped from the wagon. Chickens squawked in protest as she whipped past, scattering them with her new green skirt as she rushed into the barn. Heart heavy, Matt released the horses and followed after her. He met Emma hobbling out of the barn door, her new skirt drenched in blood.

"Emma!" He rushed to her side. "What happened?"

Her face pale and tear stained, she struggled to regain her composure, but the droplets of moisture on her lip and forehead reflected her intense suffering. "The scythe. I fell."

"Let me see." Behind her thigh, a deep gash bled profusely. "Hold your hand over it. Press hard."

"I've ruined my new dress," she groaned.

"I'll buy you another." Matt scooped her into his arms and charged toward the house, his heart thudding painfully against his ribs. What would he do? How should he handle this? There were no other doctors anywhere around, and Emma needed medical care.

He started for the bedroom.

"Not on the bed. I'll ruin the quilt. The floor is fine."

Relenting, he laid her on the floor in the kitchen. "Now, let's look at this better." Pushing away the cloth, he examined the wound. "It needs stitches."

She groaned, then set her face in determination. "Many's the time I've stitched a horse or a cow. Once I even stitched up Jeremiah. This is no different. I can do it. Boil a thread and a needle."

Matt did her bidding, all the while fighting

an inward battle. His mind fought him, but his heart dictated what must be done. When the supplies were ready, Emma sat up, twisting toward the lacerated skin.

With a resigned sigh, Matt took the needle and thread from her fingers. "You can't reach back here. I'll do it."

Tear-darkened lashes lifted toward him. "Can you sew?"

"Yes," he said tersely. "Now lie down on your belly and let's get this over with."

Bits of hay clung to the torn edges of skin, and he frowned at them, concerned about infection. After a thorough washing with soap and water, he took up the needle, working quickly, efficiently, aware that every needle prick brought her pain. Though she never complained, halfway through the procedure, she twisted her head around and watched him. Six years without practice fell away as he neatly pulled the tissues together and sealed them in a long straight line. His hands remembered what his mind had tried to forget.

"That should do it," Matt said as he clipped the last thread and wiped alcohol across the wound. At her sharp intake of breath, he grimaced, grabbed his hat, and fanned at the row of stitches. "Sorry. We don't want that to get infected."

"It's all right." Not waiting for a bandage, she rolled over and sat up, pulling one of his hands into hers. "Where did you learn to sew like that?"

When he remained silent, she turned his hand over and stroked the fingers. "These aren't a farmer's hands."

"They are now." He pulled away.

Clear, amber eyes demanded the truth. "But they haven't always been."

"No." Avoiding her gaze, he began gathering the bloodied supplies, tossing them into the washbasin.

"You're a doctor," she said simply, guessing the truth in her guileless way. "A doctor."

Apprehension flickered through him. He wasn't a doctor. Not anymore. "That's all in the past now."

"If that were true, you wouldn't still be trying to hide the facts. Did something happen? Did you dislike the work?"

Turning his back, he carried the basin to the table and stood staring at the cabin wall, remembering.

"I loved it. And I was good. So good and so confident that I thought I could fix anything and anyone." He pulled one hand wearily down his face. "I was wrong. I couldn't save the two people who mattered most to me in the entire world. My wife and baby."

She wasn't shocked, as he'd expected her to be, just full of compassion and understanding. "And you feel guilty."

"Yes."

"So you've punished yourself by leaving the profession you love. By hiding from God's call on your life."

"No!" But hadn't he? He shrugged. "Perhaps."

"Then it's time to stop, to lay down your guilt. Your skills are needed, desperately needed, right here in this town."

Even if he could lose the guilt and fear that plagued him, he'd never considered practicing medicine in Goodhope. He faced her, incredulous.

"How can you even suggest that I help anyone in that town? After the way they've treated you, they all deserve to suffer."

Emma started awkwardly to her feet, shaking her head. Rushing to assist her, Matt pulled her upright.

"When Jesus came," she said, holding Matt's hand against her heart, "everyone rejected him. He had reason to hate them, to punish them. Yet, He loved them so much — even those who crucified Him — that He prayed for them as He died."

Gripping her shoulders, Matt couldn't decide whether to shake her or hold her. "But they hurt you."

"Yes, they did. But I have you, and I have Jesus. That's all I need to be happy." Arms wrapped around his waist, Emma pressed her head against his heart. "I want you to be happy, too, Matthew. I don't think you ever will be until you can forgive yourself and resume your true life's work."

Dread rose in him like a sickness. He couldn't go back. Another failure would be the end of him.

Matt clasped Emma tightly against him, holding fast to the strength she offered. "I'm a farmer now, Emma. That's enough for me."

But the words rang false even to his own ears.

Chapter 6

A flock of geese winging its way southward caught Matt's attention as he labored in the field north of the house. He tossed a pile of fresh-cut hay into the wagon bed, then leaned on the pitchfork, gazing upward. A year ago, he wouldn't have cared about a flock of birds, but now he could enjoy the sight, thanks to Emma. The geese were the very kind of thing she loved. He thought to go and tell her about them, but before he could, the cabin door burst open and Emma rushed out.

"Did you see them, Matthew?" she called, pointing to the heavens. "They're waving at us."

Shading her eyes against the blue-gray glare, Emma hopped up and down, waving back at the honking geese.

With a smile, Matt watched Emma watching the geese. His heart filled with gratitude for this special woman God had sent his way. Her leg had healed well, he thought with relief, in spite of his concerns over infection. That was due in part, he knew, to the care he administered. He'd cleaned and dressed it three times a day, finding a measure of satisfaction in the familiar task.

Emma said little else about his abandoned profession, but she watched him with a quiet compassion that was more bothersome than nagging would have been. On the day the stitches came out, she lifted his palms, kissed each one, and said, "God has blessed you with a special gift, Matthew. Healing hands."

He'd not known how to reply. She'd asked for so little. And yet, he couldn't give her this one thing she longed for.

"Do you love me, Matthew?" she'd gone on, taking his face in her rough little hands.

"You know I do," he replied almost desperately.

"Yes, you do. But it isn't enough. You'll never be truly happy until you give in to God's calling on your life."

He'd crushed her to him, holding her against his throbbing heart, knowing she was right. The heaviness lay on him even now as the geese disappeared overhead. Emma turned his way, blew him a kiss, and started back to the house.

"Someone's coming," he called, catching sight of a copper-colored head bobbing through the south fields.

"Maureen!" Emma's bare feet churned the ground as she flew toward her friend.

Though her visits were infrequent, Maureen came when she could, bringing bits of town news but, most of all, giving Emma her friendship. While they talked and prayed, their fingers would fly: braiding rugs, piecing a quilt, peeling apples. Matthew liked Maureen as much as he disliked her father.

On his occasional trips to town, Matt was forced to patronize the general store, though he dreaded each encounter. Dreaded the arguments with Jimmy. Dreaded the thought of encountering the pregnant Mrs. O'Dell. Dreaded the longing he felt to practice medicine.

The rest of the town had warmed a bit toward him, though few ever mentioned Emma and none invited the Tolivars to social functions. He knew the other farmers helped one another during harvest. There would be husking bees and threshing parties — none of which the Tolivars would attend. He'd even had a talk with the parson, quite by accident, one day outside the blacksmith shop. Parson Jeffers had apologized for the incident at the church, saying, "The Lord would be displeased if we turn away any who seek Him, Mr. Tolivar. You and your wife are welcome anytime."

Though his anger toward the austere parson had lessened, Matt had no intention of subjecting Emma to another scene like the last.

Matt resumed the task of filling the wagon with hay, glad that the constant toil kept him from thinking too much. Another fork or two, and he'd head to the barn to unload, then start the process all over again. In the distance, beyond the acres and acres of corn and grass yet to be harvested, a spiral of dust rose. Curious, Matt paused in his work again. Two guests in one day?

A horse pounded into the yard, its rider leaping from the saddle and running toward the house.

"Maureen! Maureen! I know you're in there." The panic-stricken voice of one of the O'Dell boys carried all the way out to Matt's hay field.

Maureen came rushing out the door. After a muffled exchange of words that Matt couldn't understand, she mounted the horse behind her brother and the pair raced away, leaving Emma alone in the front yard.

Something had happened. Something bad. Matt's gut knotted with dread. Was there a sickness? An accident? Or was it the pregnant mother?

He hadn't long to wait before the questions were answered. Emma hastened toward him, hair and skirts flying out behind her. Dropping the pitchfork, he rushed to meet her.

"What is it?"

Breathless, her chest rising and falling rapidly, Emma pressed a hand to her heart. The anxiety in Matt's stomach was reflected in her face.

"It's Kathryn O'Dell. Her baby is coming now."

"Babies are born all the time." He wanted to turn away, to run back to Texas or Colorado, anywhere but here with this oppressive sense of duty clawing at him.

"Matthew, please." Emma gripped his arm. "You don't understand. It's too early, and Mrs. O'Dell is so terribly weak."

"No, Emma." Shaking his head, he backed away, knowing what she wanted. "Don't ask this of me."

"I know you, Matthew. You're a good, good man who could never live with himself if something happens to her and you didn't even try."

"How can you say that?" he cried, despairing of making her understand. "My own wife and baby are dead because of my incompetence. Don't you think I tried then? But I couldn't save them. Why do you think this time will be any different?"

"Please. Please, Matthew." Emma slid to her knees before him, the hay stubble crackling under her weight. "I beg of you. Maureen is the only friend I have."

In a posture of pure supplication she knelt before him, ripping his heart in two.

"Stop it, Emma. Get up." He gripped her narrow shoulders, tugging, but she only bowed deeper into the hay. When she began to pray, Matthew almost collapsed beside her.

"Heavenly Father, You know everything. You know why Matthew's wife and baby died. You know how he's suffered over their loss. And You know how desperately Kathryn needs him right now. Please, dear Lord, take the scales from his eyes. Let him recognize the calling on his life to minister to the sick. Give him the strength and courage to fight through this fear of failure and come out victorious. I love him, Jesus. I want him to be happy, to have the peace he lost when Martha died. It means so much to him, and he's fought it for so long. Please, Lord. Open his eyes." And she began to weep.

The gaping wound inside Matthew began to bleed afresh. He'd thought he could lose himself here on the farm with Emma and never have to think of medicine again. Instead, it haunted him, the only unresolved need in his life.

"Emma, I'll go." Bending, Matthew lifted her trembling body and held her close, murmuring against her hair. "If it means that much to you, I'll go. If you'll go with me."

Stiffening, she drew back, regarding him with anxious eyes. Though for different reasons, she was every bit as afraid as he.

"I need you, Emma. I can't do it alone."

Drawing in a deep, shuddering breath, she lifted her chin, aiming it toward Goodhope. "All right, then. I'll pray. You drive."

Drying her eyes, she clambered aboard the loaded hay wagon.

Stomach churning, pulse pounding, Matthew hammered on the back door of Jimmy O'Dell's general store, the portion of the building where the family resided. Emma stood beside him, her face pale, gripping the medical bag he'd dug from its hiding place in the barn.

"What are you doing here?" The disheveled Irishman opened the door. "The store is closed for the day."

"I'm a doctor, Mr. O'Dell. I've come to help your wife."

"A doctor, you say?" His astonished blue gaze went from Matt to the bag in Emma's hands.

"Yes. A doctor. I understand your wife is having the baby."

A muffled cry from the room's interior turned O'Dell around. "Aye. Aye. She's trying." In agitation, he ran a hand over his balding head. " 'Tis a bad time of it she's having, too. Worst I've seen."

"Are you going to let me help her or keep us standing out here while she suffers?"

"You're really a doctor, then?" O'Dell asked, his expression dubious.

"I said I was." Annoyance rapidly replaced Matt's fear. If O'Dell didn't let him in soon, he'd turn around and go home, his conscience clear that he'd tried.

"Da, what's going on?" Maureen's worried face appeared behind her father. "Emma! Matt! Whatever are you doing?"

"Claims he's a doctor. Wants to see your ma."

"For pity's sake, Da. He's the answer to our prayers. Let him in."

"It's little choice I have, but he comes alone. Not with her. I'll not have that crazy woman in my house. We've trouble enough as it is."

Matt's patience snapped. With teeth

gritted he leaned toward the storekeeper. "You self-righteous man. After all you've done to hurt her, it was Emma who convinced me to come. Now, you can either let us both in, or we'll get back in that wagon and leave you to manage on your own."

"Da, we've prayed and prayed for a doctor, and now that he's here, you're wanting to turn him out? When Ma is needing his help so badly?" Maureen elbowed around her father and grabbed Emma's hand, pulling her inside. Matt followed, feeling the anger of Jimmy O'Dell as he brushed passed.

"If anything happens to Kathryn and me babe, I'll have your hide, Matthew Tolivar. And that loony wife of yours will be locked away like she should have been long ago." His venomous tirade was cut short by a cry from the bedroom. In a rush of concern, Matt and Emma left Jimmy to fume and hurried into the bedroom where an older version of Maureen writhed on the bed.

Sweat broke out on Matthew's palms as the image of Martha flashed through his mind. If he failed again, if Kathryn died, he didn't know if he could go on.

Emma, feeling his tension, lay a hand on his. "Guide him, Jesus. Give him wisdom."

The simple prayer lifted him. He wasn't in this alone.

"Mrs. O'Dell," he said, going to her side. "My name is Matthew Tolivar. I'm a doctor. I'm going to help you deliver this baby." He turned to his two assistants. "We'll need boiled string and scissors, lots of towels or rags, and some warmed blankets for the baby."

" 'Tis ready and waiting whenever you say, Doctor."

The title sounded good, stoking his courage. He was a doctor, a trained physician with the skill to do this. Emma and Maureen bustled around the room, doing his bidding, praying out loud, while he examined the patient. To his horror, something was amiss. The baby was there, ready to be born, but even a strong contraction didn't push the infant forward. The mother worried him, too. Except for an occasional moan or the sudden arch of her body, Kathryn was listless. Her eyes were closed, her face pale and moist.

"She's give out, Doctor. I don't know how she'll manage the strength to finish."

Matt rummaged in the worn medical bag. It had been so long since he'd opened it, but the familiar tools were all inside. Struggling not to think of the last time he'd used them, he handed a pair of forceps to Maureen. "I'll try not to use these, but I want them boiled just in case."

Not every physician agreed that cleanliness was important, but Matt subscribed to Dr. Lister's notion that invisible microbes spread infection. Though he had no carbolic for disinfectant, the boiling water would help. He just wished he had some ether. Taking a baby with forceps was a difficult procedure, but under the circumstances, he was afraid it might be the only choice he'd have. Mrs. O'Dell had given up the battle and the baby would suffer damage in the birth canal if he waited too long.

Taking out his stethoscope he listened to Kathryn's chest.

"Her heart is strong," he said with relief. "If she just has the strength to help us a few more times . . ."

Quietly, Emma eased to the bedside and grasped Kathryn's pale, puffy hand. "Kathryn, dear, do you remember how you helped me when Lily was born?"

Matt's head whipped around in surprise. She'd never told him that.

Emma's sweet, gentle voice continued, "I couldn't have done it without you. Now I've come to return the favor. You're almost there, my friend. Just a little more and you can hold your sweet, precious babe in your arms."

The pale eyelids fluttered upward.

"That's right. We're going to do it together. Maureen and I will lift your shoulders and Dr. Tolivar will do the rest."

With a flicker of resolve, Kathryn nodded slightly. As the contraction began, Matt reexamined his patient, ready to forcibly deliver the child. What he felt sent a jolt of panic shooting through him.

"Stop!" he cried. "Don't push." Tension knotted his neck and shoulders. His breath grew short and perspiration bathed his face.

The cord was wrapped, not once, but twice around the baby's neck. Any further pushing would strangle the child to death. He remembered this terror all too well. Only extremely skilled hands and the grace of God could save the O'Dell baby. Matt squeezed his eyes shut for a moment.

Please, Jesus, help me to help her.

When he opened his eyes, a strange sense of calm came over him. Moving quickly and efficiently, he worked the tightly wound cord over the slippery little head with one hand while holding back the force of nature with the other. It was difficult, tedious work and time was against them.

The string of tension in the room bound

them all, so that when, at last, the noose was removed, a collective sigh of relief issued from Emma and Maureen. Matt knew better than to relax. At the next contraction, the tiny infant slid into the world, blue and flaccid.

"Oh, no," Maureen cried, hands grasping for Emma.

"Breath, baby girl." Matt ran a finger inside the lax mouth, then placed his own lips over the child's and blew gently. The baby gave a shudder, then sucked in a chest full of air. Matt swatted her bottom twice and received a mewling cry in return. The wonder of it brought tears to his eyes.

"Thank you, Jesus," Emma whispered. Matthew's heart echoed the sentiment. He rubbed the baby's back, checking her over, waiting until the even breathing and pink hues of health assured him that she was all right. Then, he wrapped her in a warmed blanket and handed her to Maureen.

"She's a little thing," he said as he turned back to the exhausted mother. "We'll have to watch her close, keep her good and warm, but I think she'll make it."

"I'll go and tell Da. He's worried sick."

During Maureen's absence, Matt and Emma cared for their patient and were immensely relieved to know that she'd weathered the delivery with no further ill effects. Rest and good food would soon have her well again. Matthew knew a sense of accomplishment he hadn't felt in years.

"I'll be back to check on you first thing tomorrow," Matt promised as he carefully placed the tools of his trade back inside the black bag. "You stay in that bed and let the rest of the family look after you for a while."

"Aye, she'll do that. I'll see to it meself." Jimmy came into the bedroom, cradling the tiny bundle in his arms. He shifted nervously from one foot to the other. "I'm a proud man, Tolivar. Apologies don't come easy. But you've got one coming, so I'm giving it to you. We needed you here today, and you came, knowing I'd fight you tooth and toenail. Still, you came. I'm grateful."

"You can thank Emma for that," Matt said stiffly, not ready to forgive the man who'd caused his wife so much grief.

"Then, I do." He turned to Emma, expression sheepish. "Maureen told me how you helped the missus. Thank you."

"I'm the one who's grateful, Mr. O'Dell," she said in her sweetest voice. "Seeing that little girl of yours come into the world was a special privilege."

Jimmy cleared his throat. When he spoke again, his voice was gruff. "If you folks want to come to church on Sunday, I'll stand up for you."

Matthew watched the change come over Emma's face. Unlike Matt, she bore her detractors no animosity, no bitterness, just a Christ-like love he still didn't understand. But after today, he wanted to learn.

By the time Emma and Matt arrived at church on Sunday morning, the service was about to begin. As they slipped quietly into a back pew, heads turned to stare. Tensing, ready to take Emma and escape before any trouble began, Matt glared back at the people of Goodhope. A few tentative smiles and a head bob here and there told him that, today, the crowd was friendly. He relaxed, squeezing Emma's cold hand. No one was going to hurt her anymore.

As the organist began to play, the O'Dell family filed in and, seeing the Tolivars, slid onto the bench beside them.

"How's your mother?" Emma whispered.

"Getting stronger. The baby, too." Maureen whispered in return.

Matt leaned forward. "We'll come by after church."

Maureen smiled and nodded as they all quieted, turning their attention to the service. The song master led them in hymns that seemed especially sweet to Matt that morning. His prayers seemed to go straight up to heaven, so thrilled was he to worship freely with other Christians and the woman he loved.

When Pastor Jeffers took the pulpit, his sermon, not surprisingly, was on forgiveness. "Now, you folks all know what I'm talking about today," he said toward the end. "We all need forgiveness from the Lord and, at times, from each other. Things have happened this week to wake us up to the fact that we've done wrong by a young couple in our community."

A few dozen pairs of eyes swiveled toward the back pew. Emma sat with head down, an almost holy smile on her lips.

"For months," the reverend went on, "we've prayed for a doctor. Finally, the Lord sees fit to send us one, and we treat his wife so badly, he's not even willing to tell us who he is. We've been stiff-necked, passing judgment on Emma, when who better to judge her mental state than a doctor who spends every day with her? If any of you still have doubts, I believe Floyd Anderson has a word or two to say about it."

Near the front, a man with a noticeable limp stood and hobbled forward. "I wasn't here the last time the Tolivars came to church, or I'd a-told this then." He scratched at his beard and went on. "All of you know the hard time me and the wife had after I busted my leg. I'm a proud man, don't like to ask for help, but if it hadn't been for Emma Tolivar, I reckon we would've starved. All them times someone saw her sneaking over to my house, she was bringing groceries. She didn't want to cause me no embarrassment. That woman's heart is gold, I tell you. She's a pure saint if ever there was one."

With an expression that dared anyone to argue, Floyd clumped back to his pew. Matt was hard-pressed not to smile at the man's feisty attitude even while he was grateful for what was said. Now, he knew for certain where Emma went on her early morning walks. No doubt, the Andersons weren't the only recipients of her generosity.

"I got something to say myself, Parson." Jimmy O'Dell rose. "Most of you have already heard about my wife and baby, and how the doctor here and his little wife saved their lives. If it wasn't for them, I'd be in mourning. That's all I got to say." With a self-conscious swipe at his nose, he sat down.

Emma's eyes shone suspiciously as she listened to the total change of public sentiment. More powerful than any medicine, acceptance was a healing balm.

"Dr. Tolivar, this town needs a man of your skills." Parson Jeffers's boots thudded softly on the wooden floor as he came to stand beside Emma and Matt. Every person in the building either stood or turned to watch. "Could the two of you find it in your hearts to forgive us? And, sir, would you consent to be our doctor?"

Pulse pounding, Matt rose to his feet, pulling Emma up beside him. "My wife is the most forgiving person I know. She's never borne you any resentment for the way she was treated. I, on the other hand, have had a bit more difficulty." He gazed fondly at his wife. "Emma here tells me I'll never be content until I let the past go and get back to medicine. Emma's a wise woman." He extended a hand to the preacher. "I'd be proud to serve as Goodhope's physician."

Rousing applause echoed through the room until the organist struck a jarring chord, then stood and said, "Thank the good Lord for that. I don't know what we'd do with all the food we cooked if you refused us. You young folks didn't even have a proper shivaree when you was wed, so we figured we'd have us a town celebration in your honor and cover the whole shebang, new doctor, new married couple, and the

O'Dells' new baby all in one whack."

The congregation laughed and began to rise, filing slowly out onto the lawn where makeshift tables were set up beneath the trees. As they followed, talking with the well-wishers, the joy on Emma's face was reflected in Matthew's heart. This was what he'd been looking for, what he'd longed for, and the crazy widow of Goodhope had been the answer to his prayers.

Filled with the kind of happiness he'd never thought possible, Matt took Emma's hand and started across the grass. Halfway to the shade trees, right in view of the whole town, Emma stopped. "Wait."

She pulled off her shoes, then whirled her husband in a circle, laughing. Matt smiled at his beautiful barefoot wife.

"You think I'm crazy, don't you?" she teased.

"That's not what I think at all."

"What then?"

"I was thinking of the day I came here, bound by my own guilty past, unable to laugh, a lost and wounded man. And you showed me a better way."

Relishing the brand of freedom she'd taught him, Matt removed his own boots and tossed them high into the air with an exultant shout. A moment of stunned silence settled over the churchyard.

"Well, what are you looking at? Ain't you all got feet?" Jimmy O'Dell plunked himself down on the ground and yanked off his boots so fast the socks came with them. With a cry of delight, Maureen mirrored her father, kicking her shoes into the tree overhead.

The startled looks turned to chuckles. Then, one by one, the people of Goodhope followed suit, discarding boots and slippers, until the whole town was barefoot, and laughing, and dancing . . . and crazy with the joy of the Lord.

About the Author

LINDA GOODNIGHT
Linda and her husband, Gene, live on a farm in the beautiful rolling hills of southern Oklahoma. Her hobbies include music, reading, spending hours in the woods and fields, and anything that involves her six young adult children. Following a serious illness which she considers a spiritual wake-up call, Linda left her dual career as a teacher and nurse. She is now in her fifteenth year as an elementary schoolteacher. Though she's published many magazine stories and won awards for her writing, *The Barefoot Bride* is her first published novella. Readers can contact Linda at gnight@brightok.net.

The employees of Thorndike Press hope you have enjoyed this Large Print book. All our Thorndike and Wheeler Large Print titles are designed for easy reading, and all our books are made to last. Other Thorndike Press Large Print books are available at your library, through selected bookstores, or directly from us.

For information about titles, please call:

(800) 223-1244

or visit our Web site at:

www.gale.com/thorndike
www.gale.com/wheeler

To share your comments, please write:

Publisher
Thorndike Press
295 Kennedy Memorial Drive
Waterville, ME   04901